Philip G. Hubert

Liberty and a Living

the record of an attempt to secure bread and butter, sunshine and content, by

gardening, fishing and hunting

Philip G. Hubert

Liberty and a Living
the record of an attempt to secure bread and butter, sunshine and content, by gardening, fishing and hunting

ISBN/EAN: 9783337294779

Printed in Europe, USA, Canada, Australia, Japan

Cover: Foto ©Andreas Hilbeck / pixelio.de

More available books at **www.hansebooks.com**

LIBERTY AND A LIVING

THE RECORD OF AN ATTEMPT TO SECURE
BREAD AND BUTTER, SUNSHINE AND
CONTENT, BY GARDENING, FISH-
ING, AND HUNTING

BY

PHILIP G. HUBERT, Jr.

"That I may accomplish some petty, particular affair well,
I live my whole life coarsely. Yet the man who does not
betake himself at once and desperately to sawing is called
a loafer, though he may be knocking at the doors of heaven
all the while, which shall surely be opened to him. I can see
nothing so holy as unrelaxed play and frolic in this bower
God has built for us."—H. D. Thoreau.
"The royal peace of a rural home."—W. S. Ward.

NEW YORK & LONDON
G. P. PUTNAM'S SONS
The Knickerbocker Press
1889

CONTENTS.

LIBERTY AND A LIVING.

THE PROBLEM TO BE SOLVED.

IT may be well to say at the outset that by the word liberty I do not mean idleness, the two having no connection in my mind. By liberty and a living, as contrasted with work and a living, I mean the getting of bread and butter, clothes and shelter for my little ones and myself by the exercise of common skill in gardening, fishing, shooting, and other out-door sports. This entails no anxious work, no tedious grind of routine in dusty towns and musty offices. It is life in the sunshine. It gives bread and butter, and contentment, if not fortune. It offers health and opportunities for intellectual recreation beyond the reach of most men under our present system. Life, to the average man, means hard, anxious work, with disappointment at the end, whereas it ought to mean pleasant work, with plenty of time for books and talk. There is something wrong about a system which condemns ninety-nine hundredths of the race to an existence as bare of intellectual activity and enjoyment as that of a horse, and with the added anxiety concerning the next month's rent. Is there no escape? Throughout years of hard toil I suspected that there might be such an escape. Now, having escaped, I am sure of it. So long as I can get a house and garden for three dollars a week, so long as oatmeal is less than three cents a pound, so long as the fish bite and the cabbages grow, I shall keep out of the slavery of modern city existence, I shall live in God's sunshine and enjoy my children's prattle, my books and papers.

For a good many years I worked hard at newspaper correspondence and miscellaneous writing without doing more than keep my family in the most modest way of life. I went to my desk early and remained late. Year after year I dreamed of the day when my bank account should be large enough to allow me at least a few months for that out-door work and sport I love so well ; yet the day of rest seemed to grow more distant rather than nearer. Grad-

ually this idea took possession of me: Why is
it not possible for a healthy man, yet strong
and in the enjoyment of youth, to make bread
and butter for his little ones and himself without chaining himself down to a life of drudgery, without passing most of his time away
from those he loves, without devoting his life to
work which is drudgery, which is hard, which
tells upon a man's vitality day by day? What
am I good for? At what work which does not
require a daily routine in a city office can I
make enough money for our simple life? By
degrees these questions began to assume a personal importance. Was it possible that I, with
my horror of the city, its bustling monotony,
its petty concern for inanities, could find work
which would offer me freedom and bread and
butter? I wanted no work which would keep
me in-doors from the beginning of April to the
end of December, no work which would every
day compel me to say good-bye to my children
in the early morning. Of course such a life
must be found in the country, if anywhere, and
in country occupations. To some people this
might mean in itself misery. To me, with
my love of sunshine, it is otherwise. During

the years when I was tied to a desk from morning till night, the very sight of the agricultural papers among my exchanges, even in the dead of winter, was sufficient to make me feel like throwing business overboard and getting into country life, even if nothing better than potato raising presented itself. At the same time that I thought and talked about the miseries of city life I was by no means blind to the dangers of the country.

Any attempt to cut loose from city life in summer might result in the city cutting loose from me in winter. Where, then, would be my music, my opera, my theatres, my lectures? As a newspaper man I had become accustomed to all these things as a part of existence. As I had lived for years in the heart of the continent's life, the quiet of a country winter might pall upon me, and when the papers brought me news of great events in the world of art I might feel that I was losing more than I had gained. And my friends and acquaintances were not slow in pointing out to me that even if I worked hard and intelligently as a farmer I could not be sure of making a comfortable living; and their picture of a farmer's life made much of early rising, long hours of work, bodily exhaus-

tion, an unceasing battle with Nature, and a
gradual relapse, intellectually, to the level of
other farmers—good men, perhaps, but dull-
witted in all matters not connected with crops
and stock. My friends predicted that a year or
two of farming would result either in the loss
of all interest in literature, science, and art, or
I would become heartily sick of country life and
eager to get back to town at any cost. I would
find, they said, that books and magazines lost
their interest after a day's work in the fields;
that gradually there would be less talk about
art and music, and more about corn and calves.
The life of hard physical labor would end in
blunting the intellectual perceptions. I recog-
nize perfectly the existence of such dangers,
and that is one reason why I should no more
think of ordinary farm life for myself than I
should undertake to compete with an Irish laborer in the raising of potatoes for market. The
question resolved itself into this: Is there an
occupation, or are there occupations, in which
a fairly intelligent man, willing to work, can
make a living in the country without resorting
to the exhausting labor of the farm, for which
he is physically unfitted? I determined to
make experiments.

YESTERDAY one of my neighbors died, killed by an accident. A rich man who, in the eyes of the world, or of that little bit of it in which we move, had attained every thing that man could wish for. Beginning life a poor boy, he made a large fortune by dealing in lard. He was looked up to in the lard trade; his judgment upon lard was final. A religious man in the hackneyed sense of the word, he had done much for the sect to which he belonged, and was cited as a model layman. He gave large sums to churches and church colleges, and contributed to the fund for sending missionaries to foreign parts. As a family man, as a husband and father, he was, for all that I know, an exemplary person. I never knew him to smile; but severity of expression may have been constitutional. With his large wealth he built himself a pleasant though commonplace home, the house surrounded by large grounds, in

6

which a dozen gardeners were kept busy. When
not too tired, it was his practice to stroll through
his grounds and garden in the cool of the evening. But his attachment to his country home
in New Jersey was not such as to keep him
from going to the city every day in the year
except Sundays and legal holidays; it was his
boast that he never took a vacation, poor man.
At half-past seven in the morning his carriage
took him to the station, and at six o'clock in
the evening it took him home again. He was
a bank director never known to miss a board
meeting; and when he died the directors of his
bank had resolutions printed in several newspapers deploring the loss which the institution
had suffered. "He died in harness," said one
of his fellow-directors to the reporter of a newspaper, "a representative American business
man. His knowledge of the lard market was
wonderful; he could give you off-hand the
day's quotations in lard for Chicago, Buenos
Ayres, London, Paris, and Timbuctoo." A
man without an idea beyond lard and discounts,
he was an important figure in the community.
Books, art, music, were nothing to him; and if
a man's name was not a good one to have upon

the back of a note, that man was not much to
him either.   The other day his coachman
allowed the reins to slip, the horses ran away,
and the rich man, in trying to get out, was
killed.

My personal acquaintance with my rich
neighbor was but slight, and of a business character.   One June morning, when all Nature
was rejoicing, it became my duty to look into
some complaints made by citizens as to stenches
supposed to come from the neighborhood of
the Hudson River at a point where several
slaughter- and rendering-houses were situated
in violation of public health and decency.   I
remember particularly that it had been hard
work for me, young and strong, fond of out-
door work in the sunlight, to leave my pretty
Jersey home that morning, to tear myself away
from my garden, with its strawberries in bloom,
from the river, upon which my little boat nod-
ded an invitation to sail ; to leave my children,
clamorous for a day in the woods or on the
water.   But duty in the shape of an investigation into these evil smells took me to the station, confined me for nearly an hour in a hot
railroad car along with some hundreds of other

unfortunates, and sent me to an unpleasant
part of the city. It happened that my rich
neighbor was interested in property in that
neighborhood; his firm bought the refuse of
the slaughter-houses, in order to transform it
into good lard. Naturally, I asked him as to
the origin of the complaints. He knew nothing of their origin, but he was quite sure that
certain rendering-establishments with which he
did business were not to blame; and to prove
it, he proposed to take me over them and show
me what nice places they were. I agreed.
When within a block of the accused establish-
ments, the stench borne on the wind was sick-
ening. My neighbor thought nothing of it; he
went there every morning, and was accustomed
to it. Having reached some rendering-cellars
beneath the slaughter-houses, my neighbor
pointed out how cleanly every thing was managed: the fat and refuse, fresh and nice, was
dropped directly from the abattoir into great
steam vats, in which it was melted. My neighbor assured me that such was the care taken
with every thing that he himself never missed
making a morning visit there. Standing in
half an inch of fatty mud and water, he sur-

veyed the scene with a pleased air, and asked
me whether I smelt any thing except the natural odors of a rendering-house.

Many times since then, when fortunate
enough to steal away from business for a few
days, and able to sail about in my boat and
teach the children how to fish, I have thought of
my highly respected neighbor, and wondered
whether he still paid his daily visits to that
horrible place. From what I know of his doings I am pretty sure that he did. " He died
in harness, like a true American," said his fellow bank directors. Very often, as I trudged
home from the river in the bright September
and October evenings, my little ones strong
with a whole day's water sport, and all of us
full of the day's joy, my rich neighbor would
be driven quickly by on his way from the railroad station. Probably he had made hundreds
of dollars that day, while I had made—what?
Had he paid too much for his money?

I have another neighbor, by no means a rich
man, and by no means looked up to in the
community, in fact, scarcely known, except to
the few who meet him out fishing, or who buy
crabs and oysters from him. He is a jolly old

negro, a man of sixty years of age, something of a philosopher, with the resources of a Yankee, and the irresponsibility of a tramp. With his wife and children he leads the life of fisherman and gardener. His nets give him all the fish he needs and to sell ; his garden patch supplies him with vegetables for the year ; in summer he is his own master, refusing persistently to work for others ; in winter he works for others if work presents itself, but as the pork barrel is deep and vegetables plenty, his actual need of money is small. Oysters he can have for the getting. This man has a genuine love of the sunlight and of untainted air. When I sail him a race for home, and we arrive wet with the spray which the breeze has thrown at us, he is the first to proclaim his keen enjoyment. He has never known what the heat and dust of a city mean ; nevertheless, he values his life almost as much as I did my brief vacations. Something also of a naturalist in his way, he does not disdain to carry home with him such queer sea products as may interest him or his grandchildren. Spending almost no money, his income is actually larger than his expenses, and he is able to pay a small

life insurance, and to put by something for the
day when oysters may be scarce or rheumatism
may get the best of him. For forty years he
has been following this life. He is not a popular man with his fellow-watermen, because
absolutely indifferent to the attractions of the
village grog-shop, and more fond of his family
than of gossip. His days are given to his garden and his fishing ; his evenings to the study
of our county agricultural journal, which gives
him, in condensed form, the news of the world
as well as the latest directions as to planting
onions.

Thinking about my neighbor who died the
other day, and my other neighbor who still
lives to catch fish and enjoy the sea breezes, I
can scarcely repress the desire to sympathize
deeply with the one who got so little out of
life. I know that such sympathy would be received by his friends and fellow bank directors
with amazement. Was he not rich and respected? Did he not die in harness? What more
can a man want? And if I timidly suggest
that there is a joy about lobster catching in an
October breeze, or even in oystering in December, far beyond the pleasure of making money

out of lard, some eminently respectable people I know will doubt my sanity. Take two men, one of whom follows the life of my late respected and rich neighbor, making existence one long strain for money, and finally dying in ignorance of every thing but the price of lard in Chicago, Buenos Ayres, London, Paris, and Timbuctoo ; on the other hand, take my poor neighbor, who, when he comes to die, will not even be mentioned by the newspapers, whose name no bank director ever saw on the back of a note, who knew nothing about the price of lard except at the corner grocery, but who enjoyed fifty years of sport, of gardening, of fishing, and of out-door happiness. Which of these two men got the most out of life ? Does the knowledge of the price of lard, or an obituary notice in the newspapers, or the esteem of Tom, Dick, and Harry atone for the loss of all sport ? Does the man who makes a fortune accomplish so much for the world that his own happiness or ease should not be allowed to weigh in the balance ? Civilization tends to the importance of the individual. The middle ages saw thousands compelled to labor for one lord and master ; to-day each man is considered

as entitled to some share of the good things in
the world, and even women and children are
coming forward. In the distant future each
man will consider that the day is made for him,
and that he who fails to enjoy himself—that is,
to use the gifts of nature rationally—is a fool.
Civilization should mean emancipation from
drudgery, and unquestionably man will some
day cease to labor in the present meaning of
the word. When machinery attains to such
perfection that the ground is ploughed, the
seed is sown, the crops are tended, watered,
gathered without the work of man ; when
power, light, heat are so cheap as to be as free
as air to every one, actual labor to provide
food, raiment, and shelter need be but slight.
At present we put a fictitious value upon labor
as a moral exercise apart from results. One
hundred years ago our Puritan ancestors doomed
here and hereafter the man who held to any
but the most dreary and dreadful beliefs ; sunlight, moral as well as physical, to them partook
more or less of the nature of sin. To-day we
are in danger of erring similarly with regard to
work. One fetish is taking the place of another. I deny that the man who prefers his

lobster boat to the banker's desk, who would rather know the habits of the clam than the price of lard in Chicago, New York, and those other places, is in danger of deterioration, or that his example is vicious. Let all the world follow your advice, say the wiseacres, and we should drift back to savagery.

That eminent financier, Mr. Jay Gould, is said to have remarked, in a fit of depression, or perhaps in an attempt to discourage envy of his millions, that his money gave him nothing more than some clothes to wear, a house to live in, and some little luxuries. Some of my critics will undoubtedly exclaim: "Look at Gould. Does he not enjoy the sea breeze in his yacht, and all the pleasures of nature?" Perhaps he does, in a difficult sort of way, filtered through flunkeys, so to speak. But of the young men who are tempted to keep their noses at the gilded grindstone, how many will attain to the dignity of a yacht? How many will die in harness long before they think it possible to stop work and begin to play? How many will lose all capacity for the enjoyment of life before their pile of gold is big enough?

ONE of the great features of most of the books in favor of living upon nothing in the country consists in the table of expenses, showing at the end of the month, or quarter, or year, where every penny has gone. I have quite a collection of such books, beginning with " Ten Acres Enough," and ending with a little volume, issued within the last year, describing how a lady managed to live in comfort and even pay rent upon an income of $150 a year. After much consideration and the preparation of many tables of the kind, showing the expenditure from day to day, from week to week, and month to month, I confess that I do not see how such tables as I can give will help any person who wishes to make the experiment. It is too much a matter of what people consider the necessaries of life. Mr. Roosevelt, in criticising " Ten Acres Enough," says that Mr. Morris, the author of that famous book, must have allowed his wife and daughters to go naked for more than five years, because, in his account of expenditure at the end of the book, not a word is said as to the cost of clothes ; which leads me to say that while I might consider myself perfectly happy with $20 worth of clothes a year, another man might think it necessary to spend $100, and his wife three times that amount. I like to wear a flannel shirt of a rough kind nearly all the year round, and although the fashion is growing, some excellent people still consider the flannel shirt a badge of social degradation. My children are dressed in the coarsest and plainest fashion, far too coarse and too plain for most city people to think proper. I work my own garden ; I sail my own boat ; I rake my own oysters ; all of which work many men I know would consider beneath them. They have no more taste for such work than for the class of books with which I occupy my evenings. My house is plain, and the living plainer. I infinitely prefer that the dinner shall be of one course, and the talk of music, books, and art, than that there should be ten courses together with inane twaddle. I once knew a family in which there were many children, where the cardinal rule at meals was that nothing must be said about the food upon the table, about the petty concerns of the house and garden, or of the people in the neighborhood. So far as possible the conversation was to be directed to some book in hand at the time, or some matter of public interest of the day. If the children were too young to take part in such talk, they were to say nothing. Of course there is a ridiculous side to any such scheme, and reminiscences of Doctor Blimber, with his maddening "The Romans, Mr. Feeder," will occur to most people. Nevertheless, there are good points about such a practice, even if it now and then leads to absurdity. If we adults are talking of woman suffrage, when Arthur, aged six years, interrupts with the remark that his goat swallowed a tennis-ball that morning, the conversation may not be so consecutive as it might be ; nevertheless, it is far better to have woman suffrage up for debate than the quality of the corned-beef or the potatoes, or the cut of Mrs. ——'s new dress. I have found by experience that systematic effort is essential in order to begin any such reform as this. As I shall have occasion to say elsewhere, without some effort, the evening, after a long day out-doors in the wind and on the water or in the woods, will prove a drowsy and unprofitable one. A few weeks' earnest determination not to let one evening pass without the reading aloud of some magazine article, or of a certain number of pages of some book worth reading, will result in permanent enjoyment ; the sense of exertion will disappear. There is a good deal to be said in favor of the life of routine in which every hour is laid out.

To return to the tables of expense again, some people might think that our bill of fare for breakfast, lunch, and dinner meant semi-starvation. We have been educated to like oatmeal, for instance, and breakfast seldom varies from oatmeal, bread and butter, coffee, and eggs. For lunch there is sometimes fish or oysters, or fruit, or a bit of cold meat. And for dinner we have fish or meat, plenty of vegetables, and, almost invariably, fruit or the simplest kind of pudding. I know that such a bill of fare would not please many people. It is low living, at all events, if not high thinking.

Probably books and magazines cost us as much as our dinners throughout the summer. Nevertheless, I have made out this little table, compiled from the expense accounts kept with scrupulous care for the eight months beginning with the first of May and ending with the first of January:

Rent (for the whole year)	$160 00
Wages	100 00
Grocer's and butcher's bill	128 00
Expenses upon garden, boat, house, including tools, paint, repairs, seeds, etc. . . .	35 00
Coal and wood	25 00
Total	$448 00

This shows a total of $448, or an average of $56 per month. To offset this sum, I have only to show as coming from the place the insignificant sum of $43, made up by sending surplus eggs to the grocer's, and giving what vegetables and hay I did not need to a neighbor. There is also a small sum to be credited to my bees. Taking the expenses of the summer, therefore, and counting the summer at eight months of the year, and leaving out the money which went for clothes, books, etc., and small extras, we have an outgo of $50 a month.

To me the life is delightful. Having $50 a
month from sources outside, there is no anxiety. I am not at all sure that even were my
$50 a month income suddenly cut off I should
not attempt to make that amount by doubling
or quadrupling the size of my garden and going into raising small fruits, chickens for market,
etc., perhaps living a little more simply than
we do now, simple as this life is.

Here I can see that my sympathetic reader,
the man or woman tired of paying out to the
landlord, the butcher, and the grocer, every
penny that comes in, tired of seeing the children
weak and puny, and anxious for a more whole-
some life than the city affords, is still dissatis-
fied. "Where," he exclaims, "even if I have
enough capital to realize an income of $600 a
year necessary for this country life, am I to get
amusement ? I must go to the city for a few
months in winter in order to hear a little music,
to see a few good plays, to see the world, to
hear the buzz of life ; my children must go to
school ; they cannot grow up fishermen or market gardeners." This is a serious part of the
problem and cannot be ignored. In my own
case it happens that I can go to the city for a

few months in the depth of winter and make enough money to pay my way during those months, going back to my country life when the spring opens. Nevertheless, after a fair trial of several years of this kind of life, much country, and little city, had I to choose to-morrow between giving up one or the other entirely, between devoting myself wholly to making every penny out of my garden and my poultry-yard, never going to New York at all, except for a day or two once or twice a year, or beginning again the city life of incessant work, of anxiety, of late hours, and bad air, with its compensations in the way of more money, better clothes, amusements—between these two lives I should not hesitate for a moment. The country life, as I make my life, gives me out-door work, which is now a physical necessity, gives me more light and air, gives me my long evenings before a wood fire, and entire freedom from worry or business anxiety.

My friends may say, and do say, that without my few weeks or months in the city there would occur inevitably a rapid deterioration, mentally. They are kind enough to hint that at present I am better than I might be. At all events, they

say, if I do not lose all interest in the higher
things of life, gradually being absorbed in the
details of vegetable-raising, poultry-keeping,
oyster-raking, and duck-shooting, my children
will suffer and sink to the level of the country
people around them. This is a serious matter.
It would be a matter of sincere sorrow to me
if my boys and girls grew up without the tastes
of educated men and women. But I do not
believe that any thing of the kind will occur.
I do not believe, as I have already said elsewhere, that a boy or girl brought up among
people who read and talk about things beyond
the village world will fail to absorb something
of the spirit of their elders. After all, are the
people of the town, taking the average merchant
and shop-keeper, so much superior to the people
of the country, taking the average fisherman or
farmer as a type? I very much doubt whether
they are any happier because they spend ten
times as much money. Certainly they are not
half so healthy, and they die earlier. It did
not need Matthew Arnold to convince many of
us that American life is often sadly uninteresting, commonplace, even inane. We all know
how sadly vapid is the talk of ninety-nine

people out of a hundred we meet.   Most of us
can count upon our fingers the men and women
we know whose talk is worth listening to.   I
am not sure that the effect of city life as seen
in our large cities is any thing to be proud of.
In the old days, before railroads and post-offices
and cheap newspapers and books, country life
meant intellectual isolation.   To-day it means
nothing of the kind; no matter how far you are
from the centres of civilization the mails bring
you all the thought of the great world worth
recording.   The conditions have changed.

People talk of the inspiration of the crowd,
the electrical influence of great numbers, the
brilliant minds reflecting light upon the dull
ones.   I confess that I can see but little of this
in our American cities.   The danger is rather
that the individual will be colored by his surroundings and reduced to that level.   Our great
public schools tend to turn out boys and girls
all knowing the same things, all thinking the
same way, all intellectually fashioned upon the
same model, and that a poor one.   Unless
I am able to provide for my boys and girls
teachers of exceptional merit, I should rather
trust to home influence and the district school

of the country village than to the great public
schools of large cities, always with the idea that
the boy would find it possible to work his way
through college some day, and that the girl
would not grow up without some idea of literature and music.   The question with me is not
whether the influence of the crowds of cities is
for good, but whether it is not for evil.

PERHAPS I cannot do better, in order to tell the sort of life that I have found possible and profitable upon an income of less than $50 a month, than to take from my diary the following record of a week. I will say nothing of Sunday, as that day is always given up by us to church-going, walking, and sometimes, in hot weather, to sailing and bathing, in the morning at least.

Monday, Sept.—Pouring in torrents ; took up a bushel of beets and a bushel of carrots and put by for winter use in the cellar. After breakfast went off in a drizzle of rain sailing with the children to Duck Island for a load of salt grass wherewith to cover the strawberry bed next December. Got enough in an hour, the children helping, to load up. The rain in the meantime cleared off, the wind coming from the southwest and cooler ; wheeled up the meadow grass from the boat and stacked it up near the strawberry bed ready for use by the

time the ground is well frozen. Wrote after
luncheon from one to three o'clock. Started
out at three for the woods with the children,
and went two miles to chop down some pines
that we can have for almost nothing for firewood. Cut up enough to make a quarter of a
cord, I should think, and got back at sundown
with enough twigs to make kindling for a week.
When my neighbor B. gets ready next month
to haul our wood-pile home, he will find that
my axe has been kept sharp. The day ended
with a splendid break of sunshine, the pink of
the whole west presaging the coming autumn.
Every blow of the axe seems to bring up pictures of what glorious good fires these pine
logs will make for us. On the way home
stopped for the mail, a bundle of books
coming from the library. After dinner read
some sketches of Henry James, published in
the old *Galaxy* years ago, which E. sends us as
worth reading. They have all James' present
subtlety with the picturesque quality that he
appears to have lost in some degree, judging
from his recent French studies.

Tuesday.—Hard work in the garden before
breakfast and until ten o'clock. Hoed up all
the bean plants and planted late carrots; doubtful if they come to much so late, but worth
trying. Had to branch up some of the tomato
vines, which were too heavy for the twigs already under them. Yesterday's rain seems to

have given a new start to the whole garden, which
last week seemed to be taking a rest after the
summer's exertions, and ready to give up the
battle for the year. The late beans, carrots,
turnips, lettuce, tomatoes looking superb.
Wrote from ten to twelve, intending to go
oystering in the afternoon with the children.
After lunch it was blowing great guns on the
bay, the white caps in every direction. Only
half-a-dozen boats out, and those triple-reefed;
too rough for pleasant oystering, and so started
off again for the woods, baby and all, the baby
going along in his carriage. Went in for tree-
cutting as if life depended upon it. Took a new
road across country coming back and got lost,
but found a deserted orchard and filled the
baby-carriage with enough stolen apples to last
a week. No letters in the mail, no books,
nothing. Finished up the *Galaxy* sketches of
James, and voted them well worth the time
spent upon them.

Wednesday.—A touch of frost in the air, although September is not half over. After
breakfast, filled up some gaps in my new strawberry bed with runners from the old one. Dug
four post-holes in order to get good stout support for the wire fence which must go around
the whole garden next year. Went oystering
after lunch with A. and L. and the children.
Delightful on the water, although towards the
ocean every thing seems to be as deserted by

the crowd as if it were midwinter. Brought back a bushel of oysters in defiance of the law, which is not yet up. Opened some of them before dinner, and packed the rest in the cellar. For dinner we had the sixth unfortunate chicken of our devoted little band. Cold enough for a fire ; we had the first blaze of the autumn, the great bunches of ferns and moss-covered twigs which have filled the fireplace all summer going first with a crackling roar. Read the last of Kennan's articles on Siberia from the *Century* and some of the "open letters." Pretty well tired out; between the effects of the fire and the oystering began to nod over our books by the time the clock struck ten.

Thursday.—Went over more than half of the garden between breakfast and ten o'clock, giving the last hoeing that will be needed this year. Notwithstanding Monday's rain, the weeds already show a disposition to stay in the ground, and it is evident that all vegetation has lost heart. Got through the task at ten o'clock, and as weeding is what I like least about gardening, there is much comfort in finding that there is such a thing as getting ahead of the weeds if you keep up the battle persistently enough. Wrote from ten to lunch time. After luncheon went with A. and the children over to the beach, sailing our three miles across the bay with a free wind in less than half an hour. One would scarcely believe that in three weeks so great a change had taken place. Three weeks ago the beach was alive with people, the bay was full of boats, sailing back and forth, the little bathing station on the beach had plenty to do, there were dozens of people in the surf and scores walking along the sands. To-day we were one of half-a-dozen sails to be found as far as the eye could reach. On the beach there was complete silence, except for the boom of the surf and the pipe of an occasional quail. Tradition says that the quail along this narrow line of sand, which stretches from Fire Island to Quogue, came ashore from an English vessel wrecked off Moriches many years ago. They were intended for some rich man's estate, but escaped here and have done well. The season is so nearly through, so far as bathing is concerned, that we gathered up our bathing suits, camp-chairs, and beach-shades, and put them aboard the *Nelly* for home. The sail home against a brisk, steady northwest breeze was one of the most delightful we have had this summer, the nose of the boat plowing the water half the way back, and the main-sheet wet half up the mast. As is so often the way on the Great South Bay, the wind died out at sundown, and as we carried our beach traps up to the house the whole west was aflame, the air cooler, but the wind gone. The last of the hotel and boarding-house people seem to be going, so that we shall soon have the bay to ourselves. One storm in early September seems to scare the whole crowd off. Had another fire after dinner, and read the last instalment of Howells' novel in *Harper's*.

Friday.—Opened a lot of oysters before breakfast and dug the other post-holes before lunch, making a long morning's work as I have no digging apparatus fit for the job. Let the chickens out for a tramp over the garden, keeping the children to see that they did not get into the tomato vines. The children picked all the tomatoes for the yearly canning—more than three bushels. Wrote after lunch until three o'clock, and started out with the whole family to go down along the shore about a mile from here where there are some branches of dead pine overgrown with silvery moss; took a saw along and brought home a lot with which to decorate ; picked up some wonderful grasses of a kind unknown to me, which we found growing to a height of seven feet in a sort of half swamp, half bog. Growing dark early, but not cold enough for our fire. Looked up and read some chapters on wild grasses, and wrote some private letters. S. gave us some reminiscences of " Die Meistersinger," on the piano, and A. sang some Schubert songs.

The talk this evening ran upon the future of music in New York, and while in J. we had a devoted believer in the grandeur and importance of our musical future, S. was entirely

sceptical, and believed that whether or 'not
the Wagner wave had a more solid foundation
than passing fashion, the real love of music was
not deep enough to encourage the hope of a per-
manent opera, such as exists in Vienna, Berlin,
Munich, and half-a-dozen other German cities.
The idea that the love of Wagner's music is, so
to speak, fictitious, and the professions of the
Wagner enthusiasts merely due to the extrane-
ous influence of the moment, I hear a good deal
about, but can never take quite seriously. One
of my friends insists that the more violent the
craze for Wagnerism, the sooner it will be over,
and that the very persons who are now decry-
ing every thing but Wagner, will soon be hailing
the advent of some new light, more abstruse
and bizarre than the Bayreuth master—perhaps
Ching-Chang, with his orchestra playing in half-
a-dozen keys at once. I know that this is a
common impression among unmusical people.
But I see around me so many persons who are
perfectly sincere in the pre-eminent position
which they gave to this music of the future,
so-called for many years, and now so much the
music of the present, that I have long ceased to
have any misgivings about the matter. The
time was when, with the neophyte's ardor, I was
ready to ascribe all opposition to Wagner
either to ignorance or dishonesty. Since then,
I have met persons who know something of
music, and yet prefer Mozart, Beethoven, or

Brahms, to Wagner, and of their honesty I am
as well convinced as of their knowledge and
good-taste. Nevertheless such persons are
very few, and whereas among musically educated men and women the preference for Wagner's music above all other is overwhelming,
the chief opposition is really due to simple
ignorance. As for argument upon the question,
it is very much like arguing as to religion ; we
have no scientific data to start from. I may
insist that the " Meistersinger " prize-song is
better music than " Silver Threads among the
Gold," but beyond quoting expert opinions in
favor of my opinion, what is there to say?
Musical judgment must be more or less empiri-
cal. In painting, in sculpture, in literature, there
are fixed standards; in music, none. The music
which to-day the cultivated world considers
admirable in every respect was condemned
a generation ago by experts as meaningless,
chaotic, and unworthy of serious attention. The
future of music in New York interests us here
in the wilderness to the extent that it is the
chief magnet in drawing us to the city when
the snow begins to fly in earnest. Were it not
for the German performances at our opera-
house, I doubt whether we should consider it
worth our while to pack our trunks and suffer
the ills of a city boarding-house for even a
fortnight.

For my own part, I look forward to the day

when the phonograph will come to our rescue.
Although this little instrument is yet in its
infancy, I do not see how any one who has
examined it at all can doubt its future importance.   It may be a year from now, or ten years
from now, but that some day the phonograph
will be the reader, singer, and player for the
family, is to me beyond doubt.   I have heard
results so marvellous from the instrument even
in its present crude shape, that when scores of
inventors have had time to work at it, its performances will be nothing short of miraculous.
In music, especially, it seems always to have
excelled. The first of the Edison phonographs,
which were admittedly toys, so far as talking is
concerned, reproduced singing, violin playing,
whistling, with extraordinary fidelity.   The
later instrument of to-day gives out a piano
piece so that not only all the notes are heard as
if the piano was in the next room, but even the
overtones and the after-vibrations of the
strings are distinct.   Inasmuch as it will cost
scarcely any thing to make duplicates of the
wax cylinders bearing upon them music, it will
pay to take great pains and go to heavy expense in order to obtain an original cylinder
which gives results as perfect as possible.
Rubinstein may well devote himself to playing
into huge sounding funnels, if he knows that
duplicates of the little wax cylinder at the
other end of the funnel are to be distributed

all over the civilized world, and that millions of
people now, and perhaps a thousand years
from now, will listen to an echo of his work.
This feature of the certain and almost costless
reproduction of these cylinders will cause the
search for a sound magnifier to begin again in
earnest. Some years ago Mr. Edison exhibited
an apparatus whereby the noise made by a fly
walking across a sheet of paper was made to
sound like the tramp of a horse across the
stable floor. Is it too great a stretch of the
imagination to predict that some similar means
of magnifying sound will be applied to the
echo of the phonograph?

Some day we may have our operas and our
concerts at home.

Saturday.—Delightfully cold again; and off
to the woods with the children right after
breakfast, there being no school. Worked
hard at the pines, while the young ones picked
up twigs and chopped for the kindling pile;
took our luncheon along, and ate it with the
music of the countless quail calling for Bob
White from all directions; the breeze was from
inland, but full of life, and laden with incense
from the miles of pine between here and Long
Island Sound. On our way home met S., with
a fine deer, which, to my amazement, he told
us had been shot not ten miles from us.
The idea of wild deer on Long Island would
surprise a good many New Yorkers. At the

store, where we stopped for the mail, there are
reports of ducks in plenty. A man with a good
gun ought not to starve around here. Two of
the children fell asleep at dinner, and, after a
little music, we decided to go to bed, omitting
the usual literary exercises, and rejecting A.'s
proposition to read a chapter on mental lazi-
ness. The dinner enlivened by a heated dis-
cussion over the "good gray poet," now
reported to be very low in health.

I do not know whether this little extract
from my diary gives a picture which impresses
the casual reader as pleasant or the reverse.
Not once during such a week had I to discuss
unpleasant matters, or distressingly commonplace matters with unpleasant or commonplace
people. I had earned enough money by writing to more than pay the modest cost of this
life. Every thing but the groceries and the
little meat required we had supplied ourselves
—the vegetables, the eggs, the chickens, the
oysters, the crabs, the honey, and the apples—
the last stolen. No doubt chopping down
wood, although an occupation much affected
by a famous Englishman—perhaps the most
famous Englishman—of this age, might appeal
to some of us, owing to the idiotic Anglomania

of the day, but it is not the sort of sport that
the average city man yearns for. The utilitarian part of it—a very important part of it to
me, and in fact I view all my sports from a
utilitarian point of view—certainly would not
impress the city man who rushes out of town
for two weeks of the year in order to get what
he calls recreation. Wood means good fires to
us, and good big fires are essential in our country home. I should say that we burn a cord of
wood in a fortnight, although the big fire is not
going all day; in cold weather a small self-
feeding stove hidden by a screen keeps the
living-room comfortable. I suppose I might
say the same thing in regard to oystering.
The poet's friend who found nothing in the
primrose would certainly not enjoy oystering.
For my part, oystering is one of the pleasures
of the year. It is one of my sports that I rank
highest. I sail my own boat over to a part of
the bay which abounds in oysters, and, allowing the sheet to run out, I can "tong away" on
deck, throwing the oysters in their queer growths
to the children, who throw away the shell and
refuse, cutting the oysters apart, as they grow
mainly in bunches, and piling them up in the

basket, which we carry home. Take an afternoon in October, with a good breeze blowing,
not enough to make the water very rough, and,
with my young ones as company, I can get as
much real pleasure and certainly as much
healthy exercise from oystering in the Great
South Bay as from any sport I know of. Then
there is the money value of the oysters to be
thought of. If I could not get a bushel of
oysters in an afternoon, I should have to buy
meat.

I have tried by practical lessons to convince
several city friends that there is a joy about
scraping the bottom of the sea for oysters
beyond any thing that they could have ima-
gined. I induced a critical friend of mine to
take off his coat one fine afternoon and work
the "tongs." The water was pretty rough, and
he had to jump about a good deal on deck in
order to keep his footing. I should say that in
the half-hour he played at oystering, he brought
up thirty or forty oysters. At the end of that
time he said that he would rather write a two-
column article than rake a bushel of oysters,
and he smoked cigars and threw shells into the
water for the rest of the afternoon. When

I met him a month later in the dusty, miserable city of New York, he said that he attributed queer pains in his back to that oystering experience. Some men are blind to the opportunities of this life.

" IT is fortunate," said one of my friends to whom I described my way of living, " that all people do not think as you do or the world would stand still. If we were all to shun the city, to go off hunting or oystering every day, contenting ourselves with the unambitious life you lead, there would be certain deterioration. Where would be our inventors, our great scholars, who devote their lives to incessant work, and our merchant princes who never miss a day in their counting-rooms, the men who plan vast operations and make the country rich and prosperous? " Of course this is the common argument against any such scheme as mine, and if a man enjoys the management of vast commercial operations, if he likes to telegraph here and there to buy tons of lard at a low price and telegraph elsewhere to sell them at a high price, I am only too delighted to have him do so and perhaps thereby enable me

to buy my lard a little cheaper at our country
store. By sitting in his counting-room three
hundred days out of the year and eight hours
of the day he gives me my lard a little cheaper,
and he finds pleasure in it. The operation gives
him a big stone house to live in, a carriage which
his wife rides in, for he never finds any time, an
opera box which his wife and daughters may
enjoy, for he has no knowledge of music ; he
has never had any time to learn any thing beyond the quotations of lard in different parts of
the world. If these noble men devoted to lard
and other commercial operations,—if they like
it, I am only too delighted. If I thought they
were breaking themselves down, losing year
after year of oystering and wood-cutting in
order to give me my lard one eighth of a cent a
pound cheaper than I should otherwise have it,
it would cast a shadow over my sports; I should
hate to think that I was reaping while they were
laboring.

Seriously, does any one contend that the life
of to-day is any happier, any more rational, any
more healthy, than the life in the American colo-
nies one hundred years ago ? So far as material
prosperity goes, it seems that there was far less

poverty then than now in the necessaries of
life ; the farm-houses were filled to overflowing
with good things to eat and drink. There were
few books, and if some inventors and workers
had not given up country life long enough to
invent power-presses we might not have newspapers and books so cheap as they are to-day.
But I doubt if any one thinks of colonial life in
this country as less worth living than our life of
to-day.   Certainly in New York City there was
not, in proportion to the population, one quarter of the poverty, the misery, the vice that we
know to-day.   There was not that fierce struggle for existence which blights the lives of so
many hundreds of thousands of our fellow-
creatures.

If the world persisted in playing as I do,
although few people regard wood-cutting and
grubbing in a garden as play, should we not
have had any great inventions, should we not
have had any steam-engines, or the power-press,
or the telephone ?   This would imply that the
man who devoted a large part of his life to
such sports as I do, wholly unfits himself for
other kinds of work—which I deny.   My own
work which brings me money happens to be

writing articles for which misguided publishers of newspapers pay me. I devote a certain number of hours in the week to writing, nor in my humble opinion is it the easy writing which is supposed to make such hard reading. There is no reason why other people who choose to cut loose from city life, having found its cost greater than its worth, should not employ a certain number of hours every day at the kind of work for which they happen to have a particular bent. I see already that my eldest boy will probably turn his attention to machinery, and perhaps become an electrician. It is not absolutely necessary that he should remain in the machine-shop all his life in order to contribute something to the world's stock of machinery. Some of the greatest inventions and most valuable suggestions have been made by men far away from the great centres of life.

Again, if in our bustling New York we saw that most men really do produce valuable work essential to the happiness of mankind, there might be some misgiving as to the policy of isolating one's self from the crowd and endeavoring to get as much enjoyment upon comparatively nothing a year as the millionaire may get. Who does not know that hundreds of the rich men of New York City owe their wealth to gambling, pure and simple, the rest of the country furnishing the victims and the money? Statistics show, for instance, that of all the buying and selling done upon the New York Produce Exchange, ninety-five per cent. represents gambling; five per cent. represents actual buying and selling of grain and produce. In Wall Street it is still worse. These dozens of well-dressed men, the men who own the yachts and the fast horses and the big country places, do no useful work, produce nothing, and if their business could be wiped out of existence to-morrow the world would be no poorer. Under cover of the little legitimate trading or business which has to be done in stocks or bonds, this army of gamblers grow rich upon the passion of human nature to get something without work. Every little town in the country sends its money to the great city to be matched against the money from somewhere else. These precious brokers are the bankers in the game. To pretend that the business is a whit better than gambling with dice and cards has always seemed to me hypocrisy; the man who deals in lard, honestly buying lard and selling lard, and not simply betting upon the future price of lard, may be doing useful work in getting lard where it is plenty and carrying it to places where it is scarce, and so throughout the whole range of legitimate mercantile life. The man who keeps a retail shop of any kind is of actual service to the community But the typical broker—what does he produce in the course of a year to pay for the large sums of money he receives? This is an old topic, and I have nothing new to say about it. But when people point to me as an idler, wasting my time and neglecting my opportunities, and at the same time point to my neighbor, the successful broker, as an example, I must decline to be impressed. At least, I give something in return for what the world gives me. The articles I write may be poor enough, but some people read them, and live to want to read more, or publishers would not buy them.

I have a dear friend who is a cotton-broker. He admits candidly that his business is gambling, pure and simple, but he contends that if people want to gamble, and want to pay him a comfortable income for registering their bets,

there is no reason why he should refuse. If
people do want to buy actual cotton, he will buy
cotton for them, although he would scarcely
know a bale of cotton if he saw one. But his
customers want to gamble, and pay him well
for helping them to do so. He has no taste or
love for chopping wood or raking oysters, but
enjoys sitting at a big desk for several hours a
day receiving checks from customers, paying
out the losses and the gains, and dropping into
Delmonico's in the middle of the day for
luncheon and a quiet talk about the best card in
the game to put your money on. When a man's
conscience can allow him to do that sort of
business day after day, I do not know whether
to be glad or sorry for him. Another friend of
mine, also a broker, to whom I said one evening at dinner, "You have produced nothing,
earned nothing of value to-day," replied to me :
"Yes, I have. Here is a check for $200, the
profits of a turn in wheat; it was done in half
an hour. I bought low, and I sold high."
"And," I asked, "do you not pity the man who
lost that $200, for you gave no equivalent
in work for it." This seemed to be so extraordinary a view of the matter that every one

laughed; no one seemed to have the least sympathy for the unfortunate loser in the game. Do not these things show that this speculation disease is blunting the moral sense of the community? My friend of whom I spoke first is a man to whose friendship I owe much, and for whose character I have the highest esteem. He is kindliness itself. And yet point out to him, or try to point out to him, that the life of a broker, although admittedly gambling, pure and simple, is a vicious one, and he will laugh good-naturedly, and go on with profound content upon his "vicious" course.

To state briefly my view, to sum up the gist of what I have put into the foregoing pages, what I advance and believe is that the hard-working city man does not get his rights out of life. It may be that ignorance is bliss. He may be swept so far in the wrong direction as to lose all proper estimate of the good things of this life; his ideas of relative values may be distorted. He may consider that fine clothes and a big house make up for lack of real sport; he may find more pleasure in counting bills than in sailing or walking. A misguided sense of duty may keep him all his life half-starved for rational sport ; he may, like the unfortunate person of whom I spoke at the beginning of this book, " die in harness " as a typical American. I believe that there is an escape from the anxiety, the toil, the wear of business in rational pursuits offered to us by the country, and that we can abandon the town without sacrificing culture, education, and intellectual life. I am free to admit that I should not advise any man accustomed to living in the tittle-tattle of the town, accustomed to "paddling in social slush," as Thoreau puts it, to go to the country carrying nothing with him. If a man has no resources of his own, if he finds no pleasure in books and literature, I should say beware of the country. Any such scheme as I have outlined would fail; it may be that very few men are so fond of out-door life that they would consider the loss of New York's advantages as of small account in comparison with the joys of wood-chopping and oyster-dredging. In writing these pages I have had no intention of tempting away the clerk from his yardstick or his ledger, or the broker from his office. I have simply had my say, knowing that I am in an insignificant minority. I think I have shown that bankruptcy need not result from such a course, providing there is a small income, so small that most men who reach middle age have it at their disposal. And in such a case there is the possibility of getting also out of the city some of its advantages, for there are several months in the depth of winter when there is nothing to be done, either in the way of sport or work, in the country. I have gone so far as to say that even if country life meant entire isolation from the city, and dependence for a living on the money which may be made in the country, even then there is much to be said in favor of such a move. Nevertheless, money is not plenty in the country, and if a man and his family are not prepared to live in the simplest possible fashion, and to undergo some little privations, better by far stick to the ills that they know of.

THREE years ago I made such changes in my business engagements as to begin my series of experiments. I wished to find out how far a small income of less than $500 a year would carry me towards independence of the city, its troubles and anxieties, its landlords and their bills. The question was whether or not I could so supplement such an income by manual out-door labor, as to keep my family in comfort the year round, and even provide for a few weeks of city life in the dead of winter. I resigned my city position and took a small place fifty miles from New York, where rent was cheap, the soil fairly good for gardening, and within gunshot of the water. I counted upon my garden, my chickens, and my boat for a good deal, and I was not disappointed. As in every village, the vegetables, eggs, chickens, and fish were dear when you had to buy them, partly because people have their own farm supplies, there being no regular business done in those things, and partly because the prices which obtain in July and August when the summer boarders or cottagers come to be plucked, regulate the prices of the year. In the three years that have gone by since then, the difficulties and advantages of the scheme have defined themselves. I can say that in my own case, at least, this mode of life is infinitely preferable for a poor man to any other that I have discovered. I do not say that if some great-uncle in India should leave me a fortune, I would not make some changes in the direction of greater sport and less actual labor, for there is labor in the raising of cabbages. And yet I confess that my pleasure over a fortune from the skies would be tempered with the knowledge that I should no longer take satisfaction in raising cabbages for the cabbages' sake. I might go on working my home acre, but it would be with something of the discontent with which I used to work a bedroom gymnastic apparatus in the days before I deserted the city. When I get through a hard morning's work of hoeing or planting, there is a decided satisfaction in the thought that by

this gymnastic exercise in the sunlight I have
been cheating the world out of a living.

But I cannot advise any one who does not
love hard physical exercise to attempt any such
experiment. It requires good muscles and
system, the latter especially, as I shall have
occasion to insist upon more than once in
chapters upon my garden, my bees, and my
chickens. Without system there is as rapid a
deterioration in a garden as in a business enterprise. Experience has taught me that one
hour's writing every day, or an hour's gardening, accomplished with clock-like regularity,
gives valuable results, where spasmodic work
ends in comparatively nothing. The same
rules which obtain in business life hold good in
my country work. The notion that a whole
day's work in the garden once a week is as
good as two hours' every morning, is all
wrong. I should say that two hours' work in
the garden once a day, from the middle of
April to the end of August, would result in
twice the garden produce that might be expected from the same number of hours' work
given at odd moments — a day here and a day
there. And so with every other country pur-

suit. So great is my preference for out-door work and sports over writing book reviews and magazine articles, that at first I was constantly tempted to throw down my pen and take to any outdoor work in sight, quieting my conscience with the plea that I would make up time in the evening. When evening came, the distasteful task was put off again until the next morning. Such rules as are necessary to get through a certain amount of work are absolutely essential. If one allots the hours of the day to certain work and allows no interference with the arrangements laid down, it is surprising what can be accomplished on a little country place. This sounds trite enough, and yet needs to be insisted upon. I am a thorough believer in the practice of a certain famous writer who sits at his desk, pen in hand, from nine till twelve every morning, whether ideas come or not. He searches diligently, even if he does not find, and the brain finally begins work without painful urging.

The new life has turned out so well that I have cast my lot for good in with Nature. From the beginning of April until Christmas I find health and enjoyment away from New

York. For the three months in winter we
board in the city, the children counting the
weeks in their impatience to get back to the
fields, even snow-covered fields. Had I now to
choose between giving up the city altogether
and returning to the old life of desk-work the
year round, I should accept the out-door existence without a moment's hesitation, both for
myself and my children. It was found that to
build a house such as we required was better
than continuing to pay rent, and for a year
preparations were made for this country home
which should satisfy our æsthetic tastes and at
the same time cost but little money.

The house stands upon a bluff, overlooking a
bay, which spreads east and west for many
miles, bounded on the south by a long strip of
barren sand. The water is not more than two
minutes' walk away, and at the foot of the
country road which leads down from the garden
to the beach, there is a little dock jutting out
forty or fifty feet into the water, far enough to
allow sail-boats to be drawn up to it. In outside appearance the house has something of the
English farm-house. The roof slopes east and
west from a central ridge-pole, with no break of

any kind except at the west end, where a big and square chimney-stack rises to a few feet above the level of the ridge-pole. On the cast end of the house the roof slants down over a piazza, which is always shady in the afternoons. Part of the piazza at the northeast corner is taken up with a small reception-room, opening upon the piazza, and through which people must pass in order to get into the house itself. From this reception-room portières open to the main room of the house, which is living-room, library, music-room, and every thing but dining-room and kitchen in one; when we have a crowd, it is a dining-room too. It is thirty feet wide, the whole width of the house, and thirty-five feet long. At the end opposite the entrance is a monumental fireplace, built of brick rather than rough stone, because stone is scarce in this part of the world. The opening is large enough to allow big logs six feet long to be thrown upon the fire, and at least four feet deep. Above the fireplace and the old-fashioned mantle-ledge, which holds a collection of more or less damaged bric-a-brac, is a device which perhaps only a musician would understand or care for. A broad frieze seven feet wide and three feet

high has been laid off in black mortar, and upon
this background music-staves have been outlined with small white sea pebbles. Upon
these staves is the beginning of the fire-motive
which is heard at the end of Wagner's "Wal-
küre," when Wotan, the great god of northern
mythology, calls upon Loge, the god of Fire,
to surround the sleeping Brunhilde with fierce
flames.

The plaster of this big room is purposely left
rough, and is colored a sombre red. Across the
ceiling goes a big beam or girder a foot square,
and were it not for the cold winds of November
and December, no plaster at all need have been
used. Around the whole room, in lieu of a cor-
nice, or frieze, runs a series of silhouettes of
life-size heads of friends of the family who have
been inmates of the house at one time or another. Such silhouettes, if cut out of light-
brown paper, show the profile outlined upon a
black background with extraordinary vividness;
the process of making them is so simple that
almost every one has tried it. With a candle
and a sheet of paper the shadow of a head
is thrown upon any paper screen, and a pencil
mark will indicate where the cutting is to be

done. Underneath each head is the date in big black letters, painted in with a brush. It is impossible to feel lonely with such shades, literally, around one.

At one side of the big room the staircase rises up and passes in a little gallery, almost over the fireplace. Underneath the stairs and alongside of the big chimney-place is a door opening into a very small dining-room. Right back of the main fireplace is the kitchen. The whole house measures thirty feet in width by fifty feet in length, including the piazza. The main room is thirty feet wide by thirty-five feet in length, and has windows opening on the piazza to the east, on the sea, or the bay, to the south, and on the moors to the north. Yet it is so placed that the last rays of the setting sun get into the house. On the north side of the building, which is shingled from top to bottom, and has never been painted, the storms of winter and the sun of summer gradually giving it a silver hue beyond the beauty of any artificial paint, is a tennis-court, shaded in the afternoon by the house. Back, there is a garden, small but perfectly kept up, a chicken-yard, an apiary, and other out-houses. The nearness to the sea

is hinted at by the presence of some whales'
vertebræ, in the shape of seats sprinkled around
the grounds. The orchard, which is at the
back of the lot, does not count for much except
in the matter of pears, which are wonderfully
successful in our part of the world.

Such a house as this, finished in the roughest
shape, but beautified by loving hands, and literally strewn with bits of color in the shape of a
rug here, a gigantic Japanese fan there, a palm-
tree in this corner, and no end of pottery of the
most flamboyant type, has a character which no
amount of expensive commonplace work can
give. Its glory is the size of its chief room.
There is scarcely a private house within miles
which boasts a room of that size, and with
all its roughness, size produces a good
effect. In its present shape, with the five
small bedrooms upstairs finished in the very
cheapest manner, the total cost of the house
has been under $1,600. Counting the cost of
some of the ornamental woodwork, which I
have done myself as a matter of personal pride,
perhaps the whole building might cost to du-
plicate $1,700. Yet the kitchen has all the
conveniences of a city house. The range gives

hot and cold water; there are stationary tubs; and a small wind-mill on the little tool house near the orchard pumps all the water to the tank that the house can use. As we are near the sea, it is rare that the breeze is not sufficient to turn the mill, which cost less than $200 all complete. The well is a driven one, and gives an inexhaustible supply of good water.

It is hard to give in words any thing like an adequate picture of this home. Take a hot night in summer, with the breeze blowing right across our big room, and there is no more delightful place for music and talk. Until long after dark the only light comes from the small lamp inside a big swinging wrought-iron bell which hangs in the centre of the room, a piece which I picked up years ago in a junk shop; it may have been intended for a hanging lamp, but I am inclined to think that it was originally part of the balcony railing of an old-fashioned house in lower Broadway. At all events, it serves its present purpose admirably. The opalescent glass with which it is now fitted casts a subdued light throughout even so big a room as ours. If it is pleasant in summer, it is better in winter. Upon one of our cold blowy

days in November I know nothing so inspirit-
ing as to get home from my oystering or fishing or hunting, to find the big room a blaze of
light from a royal fire of logs, the candles or
the lamps giving the right points of color
throughout, the warmth and the brightness
making a strong contrast with the cold wind
outside and the coming darkness.

The effect of such a room is due largely to
size, and next, to color. Its size would give it
a certain air even if the walls and ceiling were
of unpainted pine. But color may be called
to the rescue, at almost no expense. For the
sake of warmth in cold weather, as we stay
here until Christmas, and might want to stay
here all the year round, the walls have been
well plastered with rough plaster tinted a dark
gray, and forming an admirable background
for such pictures, skins, and bits of bric-a-brac
and color as we hang around. To plaster
the ceiling would have given an immense
stretch of plain surface almost unbroken by
light and shade, and to avoid this the beams
have been left open, with the immense girder
running across the middle of the room at right
angles with its length. Girder and beams have

not even been planed; the girder still shows
the marks of the axe, and here again rough
color comes to the rescue, for at a cost of less
than five dollars the whole ceiling has been
painted a rough brown red, giving an infinite
variety of nooks and corners in which the
shadows play. The frieze which runs round
the room three feet from the ceiling, and of the
decoration of which in silhouettes I have
already spoken, is painted very nearly black.
All the painting done in this room will last a
generation, and need never be renewed, so far
as actual effect goes. The woodwork within
reach, the doors, the floor, the stairs, the window
boxes and seats are all oiled pine, which may
be kept in admirable order at the expense of
about ten cents a month for kerosene and a
little labor in applying it. I have not yet tried
a winter in this house, but from the effect of
cold storms in the late autumn, I imagine that
it may be necessary to establish a large self-
feeding stove in one corner of the big room,
and perhaps carry the pipes across the room to
the chimney. For the heating of the upper
part of the house, I shall try, should we ever
need to live in it after Christmas, a plan which

has worked admirably elsewhere—namely, to cut square register holes in the flooring of the upper rooms and trust to the heat from the living room rising sufficiently to keep water from freezing in the bedroom pitchers. Two of our upstairs rooms are provided with open hearths, and should it become necessary to heat any one of the other bedrooms, a small stove, with the pipe running through the hall to the chimney, will be wholly sufficient. We are certain to have plenty of air in such a house, and we want it. Some statistics which I quote elsewhere from Dr. G. B. Barron, an English authority, upon the effect of living in small rooms, may be read with interest in this connection.

Housekeeping in this house has been reduced to scientific simplicity and I will venture to say that no time or money is wasted. Some of our devices partake a good deal of the pic-nic. For instance, with a view to saving all the labor possible, there is but little washing done. The children dress in flannel, and to avoid washing dishes we have found it possible to use wooden plates for certain meals, such as crab suppers; wooden plates can be bought for nothing and become excellent firewood.

In order to rent such a house in the country, if such a house can be found, which is very unlikely, one would have to pay at least four or five hundred dollars a summer, especially if it was furnished so as to be comfortable for a large family. A piano, for instance, and a good one, is a necessity with us. Good lamps for evenings, and ample fireplaces are also necessary. By making our home in the wilderness, if a lovely little village can be called a wilderness, we are able to fit it with every convenience and comfort, for such things cost but little money, after all. I do not suppose that my whole investment, land and buildings, but not including the furniture, rugs, and fixtures that were brought here from the city when I gave up work for sport, would represent an outlay of more than $3,000, and in estimating my yearly expenses, I put down rent as $150 a year, that being the interest upon this amount.

As I needed no large amount of land, for an acre suffices amply for all my purposes, I was enabled to buy almost in the heart of a village where land always has a certain value; and certainly with the improvements I have made my purchase has not deteriorated. Had I been compelled to go far away from the village, such a thing as selling out would have been out of the question, for of all the impossible things to sell, country property far from a station is the most hopeless. Not that I have any idea of selling, and I will not even give the name of the little village where we have found a home, for fear that I may be suspected of wishing to raise the price of land by singing its praises.

I HAVE tried this country life and found that it answers all the requirements of my modest way of living. In looking over my sources of income, I should place my garden first and my poultry-yard next. Of course, after some years of experimenting, I have discovered other, but subordinate sources of income. For instance, having much time upon my hand and aiming to get all the sunshine and fresh air and physical exercise that I can find during nine months in the year on my country acre, I took up a good many little schemes for money-making, or rather money-saving, for I believe that the city man who retires to the wilderness with the idea that he is going to make money there, will, in ninety-nine cases out of a hundred, be disappointed. I can save money in the country by providing things that we should buy almost as necessaries—for instance, vegetables, eggs, honey, fish, oysters,

small fruits, and wood for open fires. The man
who, having managed to obtain a little place of
his own, even if not more than an acre or two
in extent, will be singularly unfortunate in my
opinion, or will work with bad judgment, if he
does not succeed in providing for his family all
the vegetables, both for winter and summer,
that they can use, all the small fruits, all the
eggs and chickens, and, if he is on the sea-shore,
all the shell-fish that the neighborhood affords.

To go into details, and taking my own case
because, having done what I have done without
much special knowledge and no apprentice-
ship, so to speak, any one else animated with
a love of out-door work will be able to do as
much, or more, here is a list of the things which
I have been able to provide in sufficient quan-
tity for a large family: vegetables in profusion throughout the summer, and enough for a
large part of the winter; strawberries and small
fruits, more than could be used; ten times the
honey that could be used winter and summer,
the honey sold being part of the actual money
income of the year; during autumn and early
winter, all the oysters and crabs that the family
could be prevailed upon to eat, the children at

last refusing to accept oysters in any shape as a substitute for meat; all the eggs and more than could be used, and chickens for the table from the end of July until far into the winter. With the additional experience of several years of this life I find other sources of income looming up, or rather of money-saving, for I should like to emphasize the idea that it is not money-making I aim at. Some of my friends have succeeded admirably with pigeons; others have done wonders with mushrooms, an acquaintance of mine out in Jersey having paid his rent and the wages of a man out of the proceeds of one small mushroom house not twenty-five feet square. These are things for future experimenting with me, but of the others I can speak with knowledge.

At the same time I would warn any one that there is a certain amount of danger, the worst side of the picture having been set forth amusingly, although too flippantly, in my opinion, by Mr. Robert Roosevelt, in his amusing book, " Five Acres Too Much." As I have already hinted in my garden talk, there must be hard work and systematic work, and work done in person, and not by proxy. It may be said that

the hired man is the bane of every garden so
far as actual money-saving is concerned; ten to
one the inexperienced city man will find the
wages of his man about double the value of the
vegetables or fruits obtained. There are seasons
of extraordinarily bad luck in gardening—no
rain, or too much rain ; no sun, or all sun ; but
with a small garden of an acre or less the
intelligent workman is almost master of the
situation. I can point to no great money-making
operations as the result of my own gardening,
but I know of more than one instance in which
high culture of a careful and intelligent kind
upon one acre of land has produced a money
profit of $1,200 in one year.   This, to be sure,
was done in the neighborhood of high-priced
markets, and by an expert.   The secret of it,
as I learned by watching the process almost day
by day, was to allow no bit of the plot to go to
waste.   Every square foot of the 43,560 square
feet in that acre bore its crop, and bore the best
crop that could be obtained from it and nothing
else.   The secret of keeping down weeds was
never to let them get a beginning.   One man
was employed in doing nothing but stir up
the earth with a cultivator, with the result that

every bit of good in the earth and in the
manure that was put into it went into the
vegetables. You cannot raise two crops at the
same time from the same ground, and it must
always be borne in mind that between vegetables and weeds, the weeds are by far the hard-
iest and most voracious.

Mr. Roosevelt, in his " Five Acres Too Much,"
seems to have had peculiarly bad luck from
beginning to end. Every thing that he took
hold of—cow, pigs, horse, garden, fruit-trees,
strawberries, chickens—turned out badly, and
he could not find enough to say of the misery
of his experience. He admitted that he had
been led to that experiment by reading "Ten
Acres Enough." I will confess that I was led
to my experiments by the same book, but my
experience has been entirely satisfactory to
myself, and I should be sorry to think that it
was beyond me to keep a small garden in beautiful order and raise a lot of chickens.

The poultry question has been so often gone
over, and so many columns have been written
about the vast sums of money to be made by
raising poultry, by sending spring chickens to
market, or by selling eggs when they are dear,

that it is scarcely worth while to say more than a word about my chickens here. I have invariably found that the schemes of my friends who went into poultry-raising as a business, and several of them have done so, turned out badly, partly because they expected to make money out of the business instead of a mere living, and partly because the keeping of 1,000 chickens seems to be a dangerous proceeding—to the chickens. In my own case I have never attempted to have more than fifty chickens at a time. With an insignificant expenditure this flock has proved to be quite sufficient. Again this is a case where simple care and system are necessary. In the poultry-yard as well as in the garden beautiful order and precision in work pay. In our part of the country ducks have also proved to be one of the native resources, but of that I have no personal knowledge.

As to the resources of the water, every one cannot live at the sea-shore, and even at the sea-shore there is not always an oyster bed near, or clams, or even great lots of crabs. Friends of mine who have attempted for a few months something of the same life that I lead nine

months in the year and have pitched their tents
on the Massachusetts coast, really seem to get
more out of the water than out of the land.
They get an extraordinary number of fish, lob-
sters, and clams, they get sea-weed which they
use as manure, and scarcely a day passes but
some kind of sea food does not make its appearance upon their table. I have never been
so fortunate as to be placed where the fishing
was of such a nature that I could depend upon
it from day to day to furnish the table. Nevertheless, I have no doubt that during the summer and autumn I have provided more than
fifty dollars' worth of good fish of various kinds,
and I leave out of account entirely the oysters,
because they can be had for almost the picking
up where we are. With us the bay furnishes
perhaps the most valuable manure to be found
along the coast—the bony fish which the fishermen get in their nets in enormous quantities
and either sell to factories where the oil is
squeezed out of them or throw them on the
land to be used by the farmers as manure.
Making a liberal estimate, I should think that
the actual money value of the fish, crabs, and
oysters that I get during the summer must be

at the least one hundred dollars, and this is sport, as many city men will admit, and none the less sport because done week after week, and not during a few days' escape from the city.

I still remember with something like enthusiasm the impression that the famous book— much ridiculed but nevertheless of serious value to so many persons—" Ten Acres Enough," made upon me many years ago. At the time when I came across it by chance I was very tired of city life, of late hours and long hours, of nervous strain, of incessant work with few breathing spells. My routine at that time consisted of steady labor from nine o'clock in the morning until twelve o'clock at night with very few intervals for rest and recreation. And then it often occurred that work which had to be done took me out of bed long before daylight. Four years of this sort of drudgery with very small prospects of release in the future or of reward which would have made such toil bearable, often caused me to turn over in my mind whether there was not some avenue of escape. As country pursuits had always had a fascination for me from childhood, I had heard more

or less of the famous "Ten Acres Enough."
One night as I was leaving my office a friend
presented me with an old copy of the book,
which he said would interest me as I was fond
of preaching upon the superiority of country
life to city life. On the way home I opened it
with but small expectations that any thing in
it could apply to my own case. With all my
love for the country and for country pursuits I
had never thought of myself as a practical
farmer or of the possibility of making any kind
of a living out of the soil. It has been pointed
out to me too often that while potatoes and
cabbages are raised all about New York by
men who make a poor living at it, any German
or Irishman just landed at Castle Garden could
raise more potatoes or cabbages than I because
he would have more muscle to put into the
work.

Many of my readers may happen to know
that "Ten Acres Enough" is the record of the
successful attempt of a Philadelphia merchant
to support himself and his family by raising
strawberries and other small fruits. Middle life
had found him no nearer fortune than when he
began ; he felt that strength was ebbing away

and he was losing enthusiasm; business cares
were becoming thicker rather than otherwise.
Notes had to be met which caused him constant
anxiety. He could take no pleasure in life. One
day a friend suggested to him to drop the whole
effort for a fortune and try for a comfortable
living in quieter, less ambitious, but safer fields.
He took the advice and sold out his business,
realizing two thousand dollars, with which sum
he bought a little place of ten acres eight
miles from Philadelphia, and planted it mostly
with strawberries. The book gives the results
of five years' work, with figures showing exactly
what money came in and what went out. At
the end of the five years he had recovered
health and spirits; he had kept his family in
comfort; he had lived an out-door life of far
more interest to himself than any business life
could have been; and he found his property
more valuable and his bank account larger than
when he began. I confess that once having
plunged into " Ten Acres Enough " I read the
book through with more eager interest than if
it had been the most absorbing novel. Here
was what I had been looking for. I loved sunshine, I was fond of gardening, I had a passion

for grubbing in the earth, for watching things grow. I have had many years of city life, and far more than my share of city amusements as my connection with newspapers has supplied me with tickets to all places of entertainment. I said to myself : "This is the life for me ; I will raise strawberries, raspberries, blackberries, and other pleasant things, and if I do not grow rich I shall at least have strength and health wherewith to enjoy the sunlight and the country air."

For months this idea haunted me without taking practical shape. It is no easy matter for a man absorbed in professional life, especially newspaper life, to get out of it, and without capital as I was, the notion had something unpleasant about it. To cut loose from an assured income was dangerous. The strawberries might not grow, the drought might kill my blackberries, there might be a glut in the market when I came to sell, even if I had any thing to sell. I might get tired of solitude, and might yearn for the nervous activity of the city again. I might come to think that a good opera was worth a million strawberry plants, and the end might be—as most of my friends predicted—

that I should sell my ten acres at a tremendous sacrifice, and take up my newspaper work again under greater disadvantages than ever. Nevertheless, so firmly was I convinced that there is a joy in gardening well worth striving for, that when spring opened I took a little house in New Jersey and began to feel my way along. I was quite convinced that for a man who knew nothing about gardening except theoretically, only failure would result from burning my ships behind me at once. So I kept on with my work in the city, but moved out to the country, taking a little place with a small garden. Meantime I bought every popular book bearing upon the subject of gardening, and I subscribed to several agricultural newspapers, which I read with conscientious thoroughness. I have quite a little library upon agricultural matters, collected that spring and summer.

My garden, to begin with, was in the most rudimentary condition, having been allowed to run to grass. After digging up a spot about ten feet square in the turf, taking the early morning for the work, I decided that it would require all summer to get the garden fairly spaded up, and so I hired a stalwart Irishman to do the work for me, which he did in a week, charging me nine dollars for the job. As he professed to be also an expert in planting vegetables, I bought a supply of seeds in the city and entrusted them to him, assuring myself that once in the ground the rest of the work would fall to me; if I could not keep a garden patch fifty feet square clear of weeds, I had better abandon the business at once, and all hopes of making a living out of scientific gardening. The beginning was an unfortunate one. The weather happened to be first very wet, and then so dry and hot that my vegetables were unable to break their way through the baked earth. When my peas and beans still gave no signs after being in the ground two weeks, I discovered that the whole work would have to be done over again. A Presidential campaign was beginning which kept me in town often late at night, so that the chief labor of the garden fell to my faithful Irishman, who got far more satisfaction out of it than I did. The vegetables finally did come up above the surface, and many an evening I finished a hard day's work by pumping and carrying hundreds of gallons of water to pour upon potato plants,

tomato plants, bean stalks, and other things
which a friend of mine, an expert in such
matters, assured me were curiosities of mal-
formation and backwardness.   My Irishman
told me that it was all for want of manure, and
by his advice I bought six dollars' worth of
manure from a neighboring stable, and had it
spread over the ground.   The bills for my garden were meanwhile mounting up.   I had
begun the spring with a garden ledger, keeping
an accurate account of every penny spent, and
hoping to put on the other side of the page a
tremendous list of fine vegetables.   The accounts are before me now, and I presume that
every one who has been through the same experience has preserved some such record.

The tools, rakes, forks, spades, hose, water-
ing pots, lawn-mower, etc., cost me $18.
Wages to my stalwart friend during the
whole season were $26.00; seeds were $2.80,
manure, $6.00; wire fencing, made neces-
sary in order to keep out a flock of my neighbors' hens laboring under the idea that in
my garden were to be found the best insects
of the whole neighborhood, and acting upon
this belief, $5.00—total, $57.80.   Of this

amount the tools and the wire fencing—say $20—may be looked upon as well invested for the future, so that my actual outlay, for which I should receive an equivalent in the shape of vegetables, was about $37. The list of vegetables begins with entries day by day; then the garden produce is lumped at the end of the week; and finally in September the garden appears to have yielded nothing but tomatoes and beets, the potatoes having failed to come to any thing, owing to a variety of causes, which my assistant explained in different ways on different occasions. One day he said that the potato bugs had done it, and another day he was convinced that if I had put in manure enough earlier in the season I might have had splendid potatoes. In other words, if I had spent ten dollars for manure, and had given up my days to fighting the bugs, I might have had five dollars' worth of potatoes in return.

The first entry of vegetables is in a bold hand, and is to the effect that on the 10th of June we had some radishes of an estimated market value of five cents. Then come lettuce and peas, and later on spinach, beans, radishes, carrots, and finally tomatoes in profusion. For

some purpose which I could never fathom, half
of my garden plot was planted with cucumbers
of a particularly hard and leathery type. They
throve in the most wonderful fashion, and there
were bushels of them, of no earthly use to any
one ; we could not eat them or give them away.
They rotted where they grew, and seemed to
serve no purpose except perhaps to enable my
assistant to point to something in the garden
which looked like a successful vegetable. To
be brief over a somewhat painful experiment,
and estimating the garden stuff that we really
got out of my little plot, I should say that delivered at our door the stuff would have cost
us not more than $15, or about half its
actual cost. I do not take into account
the value of my work in hoeing up tons of
weeds and pouring down tons of water, because
the practical knowledge I gathered more than
offsets these tremendous labors.

In the meantime I had profited by studying
neighboring gardens, notably a very beautiful
one belonging to a neighbor who did all the
work himself and produced a crop of vegetables
which seemed to me nothing less than miraculous. Every inch in this neighbor's garden

seemed to grow something ; his vegetables took up so much room, were so close together that the weeds had not a chance to squeeze themselves in. He worked upon the theory that one square foot of garden properly manured and properly attended to was more productive than four square feet half taken care of, and his results proved the soundness of his ideas. It was owing to this neighbor's advice that my second summer's work in my little garden, for I was determined not to give the ground up although it had proved a costly toy, were far more satisfactory in every way than the first. I discovered that my neighbor's total expenses of the year for his garden, which was a far larger one than mine, were less than $10, nine tenths of which sum went for manure. He did all the work himself, got his seeds and plants from neighboring gardens, and the value of his product exceeded $100 during the summer. This was something like gardening, and if one man not a Hercules could do it, why not I ? My second summer showed that by devoting an average of two hours a day to my little garden patch I could save about fifty dollars in the vegetable bill of the family. Estimating

that the garden work begins on the 1st of May
and ends on the 1st of September, we have
four months, or 120 days, during which I gave
two hours a day, or 240 hours, to my garden.
At ten hours a day this represents twenty-four
days or a month's work. At my regular profession I can make $200 or more during the
month, so that at first view the occupation of
raising vegetables does not appear well, finan-
cially speaking. Upon the other hand, considering that these two hours a day were to me
hours of genuine enjoyment and that the work
unquestionably did me good in every way, I
can say that the garden was a success.

A good many years have passed since I
began my little garden out in New Jersey. In
the course of events I found myself compelled
to give up playing at garden and to move back
to New York. Newspaper life takes all or
nothing out of a man, and I was by no means
ready or able to neglect serious work which
paid me a very fair living in order to amuse
myself in a Jersey garden. But during those
years of experiment I had learned a good deal
about practical gardening. I learned enough
to know that with less than three hours' work

a day I can provide a good-sized family with
all the potatoes, cabbages, turnips, carrots,
onions, and beets that will be needed the year
round ; all the raspberries, blackberries, strawberries, and currants for the summer ; all the
peas, beans, beets, lettuce, spinach, and tomatoes that will be needed in summer. And I
can do this with an expenditure for manure
not exceeding $12, provided the ground is in
reasonably good condition. I think that the
reader will admit that this is something well
worth knowing. The trouble with most men
who go into gardening upon a small scale is
that they pay out money for what they should
do themselves to men who are often lazy or
dishonest, and that while they themselves may
work very hard for a few hours or a few days,
the work is intermittent, and that is the worst
sort of work for a garden. With a garden, the
maxim, " a stitch in time saves nine," is particularly true. I have seen pieces of ground in
such a condition that in half an hour's work
with a steel hoe I could kill every weed there ;
three weeks later to do the same thing would
have required a day's work or more, and then
it would not have been well done. To manage

a small garden scientifically is a matter for the most systematic kind of work. Three hours a day of steady work upon a plot 100 feet square will give every thing that can be wanted in the shape of small vegetables. If potatoes and cabbages are required a larger patch will be needed, but even then systematic culture will tell wonderfully. The use of new tools, such as the hand cultivator, which does more work in half an hour than can be accomplished with a hoe in two hours, has greatly simplified the raising of vegetables in a small garden. It is also more than true that one square foot well cared for is equal to three times the area half cultivated.

Still another source of income which has been suggested to me by my tramps around the country, and a business which offers no extraordinary difficulties to the inexperienced, is the raising of fine fruits for our New York market. We have scores of farmers in my neighborhood who make a living, and a comfortable one, from their fields and their orchards, and trust almost to luck for the quality of what they have to sell. I have been struck many times with the wonderful return for care and manure made by

several species of pear-trees that flourish on
Long Island. For the city beginner to undertake to raise apples, or strawberries, or common
pears, or in fact any orchard or garden produce
common in the markets, is to experiment
against heavy odds, as he will come in compe-
tition with men who have been at it all their
lives. At the same time, perhaps he will succeed, owing to better methods and less dependence upon routine. But what I should
advise the city man who wants to make some
money out of his six or eight months' work in
the open air, is to try for something not produced by his neighbors, or not produced in the
same way. For instance, there are new kinds
of pears, which grow profusely in parts of Jersey and in parts of Long Island, which nevertheless still bring a large amount of money as
compared with apples or ordinary pears. I
should advise the city man to go in for culture
of this sort, devoting himself to an orchard of
half an acre, if he cannot keep any more trees
in perfect order. I have seen such astonishing
results from these new species of pears, that
were it not easier for me to make more money
by one hour's writing a day than by ten hours'

work in an orchard, I should certainly go into the business. So much is said about the impossibility of making any money at gardening or fruit-raising that it is almost hopeless to convince any one to the contrary, and it is far from my wish to do any thing of the kind. My aim is to tell how I manage to do without money, not how to make it. The first is a topic upon which I have had some experience, for reasons beyond my control, while as to the last I cannot speak as an expert. The scores of books which prove that if a man can raise ten thousand quarts of strawberries from an acre of ground, and sell them at ten cents a quart, he will grow rich and his family will rejoice, are mostly based upon the experience of some wonderfully clever person; the truth of their theory is irrefutable, provided you admit the premises. They remind me of a circular once sent to me by a man who was offering fame and fortune in return for ten cents in stamps. He set forth that if I bought from him a certain prescription for a magic hair-grower, to be manufactured at four cents a bottle, fortune was mine. For if I sold ten thousand bottles of the stuff to agents at fifteen cents a bottle, who in turn would sell it at twenty-five cents a bottle, I would make eleven hundred dollars, the agents would make a thousand dollars, and the whole neighborhood would rejoice, except perhaps the bald-headed man who bought the magic restorer. I can tell people how not to get rich at newspaper writing, but I am not yet ready to offer any advice of the sort given in books patterned after " Ten Acres Enough." My ideal orchard is one given up to trees and grass, and used for poultry until the fruit begins to fall. The trees, the grass, and the poultry are all pretty sure to thrive with the most ordinary care. The chickens kill the worms, and the hay crop will more than pay for all the labor expended in taking care of the trees. As in a garden, my experience has been that the very best results in an orchard are to be obtained by the highest culture of small plots. Two apple-trees of a good sort, kept well pruned, well manured, and free from insects, are likely to yield as much fruit as half-a-dozen neglected trees, and the picking will not entail half the labor. I see the same advice given every day in agricultural papers and books throughout the country, and yet for

some reason a really well kept orchard, with all
the trees in prime condition, the fences in neat
repair, and not a superfluous twig to be seen, is
one of the rare sights of the country.   It is also
the commonest sight to find upon one farm a
few trees which give a splendid grade of fruit,
while the next mile or two will show nothing
but apples or pears scarcely worth the picking
—all because the man who planted would not
take the trouble to pay a few cents more in order to get choice stock from a good nursery.
Of all the economies that pay least, is the
saving of a few dollars in stocking a young
orchard.   I have talked with many of our
farmers about this, and almost invariably the
blunder is due to small economy; they got
their trees from some one in the neighborhood
who sold cheap as compared to the prices of
first-class nurseries, and, as a result, year after
year, their orchards gave them half the returns
which would have been received from good
trees.   My ambition is some day to prove by
dollars and cents that it is not impossible for a
city-bred man fond of country work to make
money in an orchard, for nothing that I have
heard to the contrary (and every friend that I

have warns me of the futility of such an attempt) has convinced me that starvation lurks everywhere but in the dust of the city or the turmoil of trade.

BESIDES my oystering, the fishing that I
have done has proved to be of no small
value as part of our scheme. Unfortunately,
since settling down by the water the fishing appears to have become somewhat scarce in my
neighborhood as compared with former years.
Forty years ago, so old men tell me, the whole
Great South Bay was full of salt-water fish;
there were inlets from the ocean at several
points between Fire Island and Moriches, and
the sea-water ran in through deep channels
which years ago became choked up with sand.
To-day there is no opening in the Great South
Bay to the ocean except at Fire Island. At the
other end of the bay, twenty-five miles eastward, the water has become so fresh that clams
will not live in it, and most fish are shy about
going so far from deep water. Nevertheless,
we catch crabs by the hundred, and in the
autumn many young bluefish, known in the

neighborhood as "snappers." Once a week I sail my boat down to the neighborhood of Fire Island, where from June to November we get some good bluefishing, thanks to our "chumming" machines, a device for chopping up bony-fish in appetizing shape. The boat is brought to anchor, the sails furled, and this chopped fish is thrown overboard in small quantities. The bluefish, running in or out with the tide, are attracted by the "chum," and come to feed. The hooks are baited, and thrown overboard along with the chum. If fish are plenty, the piece of chum which hides a hook is sure to be snapped up. When bluefishing is fair in the Great South Bay we can count upon a catch of from twenty to thirty fish, ranging from one to five pounds. But bluefishing is an uncertain sport. I find from my diary that out of twenty trips to Fire Island, eleven produced nothing, except that each trip gave us ten or twelve hours of glorious sailing. An advantage of this bay for sailing over any other that I know of, is that if rough weather comes on the little craft can take shelter at any of the many villages skirting the bay, and the fishermen can get home by train if it is necessary. There is always a safe harbor within twenty minutes' sail.

Our crabbing is enough of a resource to be worth writing about. After August it is at its best. Then the few summer boarders and cottagers who linger after the middle of September join with the native in hunting the scavenger of these waters, counting a day lost which does not bring at least a score of big crabs to an end, which I hope is not " something lingering." As an earnest believer in the value of the late Mr. Bergh's work, I have tried to find out by experiment exactly how lingering is the death by boiling water to which the crab's preference for stale fish and other bits of kitchen offal finally brings him. Repeated experiments show that death is almost instantaneous, if it is true, as is so often said, that a crab lets go his hold only when dying. In order to clear one's conscience upon this matter it is necessary to submit the crab to what may be extremely painful proceedings. Let a strong crab get a good hold upon a piece of rope or any other soft material not too intimately connected with yourself, and lower himself slowly into boiling water ; the crab will let his claws and nearly half of his body get parboiled before he thinks of letting go. Instead of this, begin by plunging the crab instantly under, and the claws open at once. The notion that it is more humane, as some people contend, to half pulverize the crab with an axe before boiling him, is the sheerest nonsense, as any one can find out by experiment.

The last year has been an excellent one for crabbing—a better catch has not been known since 1876. Earlier in the season, before the first crabs had made their appearance, an old "Cap'n" and fisherman of this neighborhood, who is an expert in all matters pertaining to fish, tides, weather, and profane language, told me that there would be no crabs this year. He is a dear old man, close upon eighty years of age, who is so full of gentle humor and kindly shrewdness that he can rip out oath after oath without offending any one. "He swears so gently," said a lady of my acquaintance, "that it does n't seem like real swearing."

"That 'ere —— blizzard," said the old fellow to me one evening in June, as we sat on some eel-pots discussing the next day's weather, "killed every —— crab in the bay, sure. The

—— ice hurt 'em ——, and then the —— blizzard made the water so cold that the ——
critters all died. You wont see a —— crab here
this summer."

But it seems that the crab crop is somewhat
like the peach crop. The regular spring an-
nouncement to the effect that every peach-bud
in the country has been nipped by the frost is
hailed with joy by every lover of peaches, who
then feels sure that a fair crop can be counted
upon. The blizzard may have done many
things; it certainly did not kill all the crabs.
It knocked down the docks of the neighborhood, and put back the spring about a fortnight;
it did all sorts of damage to chimneys, roofs,
and fences. But it did not kill the crabs, and it
gave an inexhaustible topic of conversation to
the gentry who gather around the store-stove
six nights out of the seven to settle the affairs
of the nation, if talk can settle them. If the
fish did not bite ; if the summer was windy and
cold—which it was ; if the surf was dangerous,
the apple crop poor, and the potatoes rotten,
the fault was laid to the blizzard, that awful
visitation, when, as the Cap'n says, " New York
did n't hear from us for more than a week."

The crab is a stupid fellow about the traps laid for him, and when hungry will hang to a bit of fish even when lifted half out of water. The later the season and the bigger the crab, the more certainty that no crabs will escape. I suppose that we catch our crabs in about the same fashion that crabs are caught everywhere; tie a piece of fish or meat to a string, throw it off a wharf or off your boat, and wait for a bite. The crab, prowling about the bottom, seizes it with his nippers, and begins his meal. By raising the bait a few inches from the bottom, a person can tell, after small experience, whether a crab is around or not. If the crab likes his fare, he will hold on until he is drawn well up to the surface, when, with a deft movement, the scoop-net is run under him, and all is over for that crab. All kinds of bottoms seem to suit him—sand, mud, even eel-grass. When caught in a calm and able to drift slowly over the flats which extend for a mile or more into the bay from the narrow sand strip which separates us from the ocean, one can catch crabs by the dozen if quick with the net and not too afraid of falling overboard. The favorite *habitat* of the beast, however, is the channels which skirt

the shore, especially where the offal from board-
ing houses or hotels is thrown into the water. It
is counted poor sport when an afternoon's crabbing does not produce thirty or forty crabs.
On calm days, the boys often catch their bas-
ketful by watching the water along the sides of
the docks; the crabs swim on the surface in
search of the shrimps and minnows that hide in
the grass and sea-weeds that grow upon the
spiles.

The money value of the crab, even here,
where they can be caught by wholesale, is
sufficient to cause many of the fishermen to
make a business of "shedding" them in confinement. Fair hard-shell crabs are worth, even
upon the dock here, thirty cents a dozen, while
for "shedders" or soft-shells, a dollar a dozen
is not considered exorbitant. This high price
of soft-shell crabs has resulted in a regular business of keeping in floating boxes or "cars" such
crabs as are about to shed their shells. An expert can tell the crab that is going to shed almost without looking at him. By dint of ques-
tioning every man within two miles of here who
owns a car I think that I can tell some crabs
that are going to shed. To the inexperienced

all crabs look alike ; they are crawling creatures with a surprising grip. Few persons, and no women, ever get near enough to a crab to admire his superb coloring and the delicacy of his work upon a piece of old fish. But the student who has listened to a dozen life-long experts and has tried to reconcile their wholly opposite accounts of the nature of the animal, know that there are crabs and crabs. Turn a dozen crabs over on their backs and they may easily be divided into three classes. One set will be perfectly white, with the "breastbone" or plate, a narrow strip ; another set, having the breastplate expanded so as almost to cover the whole shell and streaked in dark blue and green ; still others have the narrow breastplate, but the whole under part of the crab is discolored and not a cream-white. The first class comprise crabs that have already shed this year and have grown hard. The second class are the "pocket-books," as the fishermen call them, crabs that will shed no more ; and the third class are those which may shed their shells this year. For eating, the crab with a cream-white color upon the underside is most esteemed. All the very large crabs are likely to

be " pocket-books," but some that I have eaten
were quite as good as any of the white fellows.
An expert can tell by squeezing the crab
whether the shedding period is near. If within
a few days of the time, the crab is put into a
car with others supposed to be in about the
same condition. It might be thought that
soft-shelled crabs ought to be cheap if they
can be hatched out in this easy fashion. The
trouble is that eternal vigilance is the price of
the soft-shell crab. Every fisherman has to
watch his crabs night and day if he wishes to
save his soft-shell crabs from being eaten by the
other crabs. Until within five hours of the
shedding, the crab retains his activity and vo-
racity, when he will fall upon any thing eat-
able ; then comes a period of stupor, and then
the old shell is thrown off, leaving a perfect
crab, one size larger, but soft and helpless. If
all the other crabs in the box are not equally
helpless, the new soft-shell fares no better than
in Washington Market. My friend, the Cap'n,
examines his crabs at six in the morning, at
noon, at six o'clock at night, and often again at
midnight, when he has a large number of " shedders " on hand. Moreover, a crab gets hard so

quickly that for market purposes he should be taken out of the car and packed in sea-weed the moment he sheds. In five hours after shedding, a crab, if left in water, becomes a "leather-back" and of no value, comparatively speaking. There is one man near us who, with the aid of his two boys, sends to market more than a hundred "soft-shells" a day in the season. The artificial propagation of crabs in shallow salt-water ponds has been tried here, but abandoned, owing to the regularity with which the crabs devour their young when they can catch them.

Cooks seem to differ as to the right time which a crab should boil. Expert opinions vary from five minutes to half an hour. I am inclined to think, after many experiments, that twenty minutes is none too long, and that half an hour's boiling does no harm. If the pail of crabs is lifted to the edge of the pot of boiling water, and slightly tilted, the crabs will walk to their own death upon hearing the bubble of the water. Thus it is pleasant to think that the crab's last impressions may have been a satis-faction to him ; the gurgle of water is in his ears as he takes the plunge, and before he discovers that he is not in the Great South Bay all things are indifferent to him.   The change of color from dark-green and blue to cardinal-red takes place the moment after the crab is in boiling water, and is no indication that he is cooked.   Those persons who know the cooked crab only have no conception of the superb coloring in green, turquoise-blue, and ivory-white which makes a live crab a thing of beauty.   Crabs in market are so often cooked in order to keep them the better, that it is no wonder some people imagine that the crab goes through life in a scarlet coat.   I saw last winter a game picture which had, among other things, a bright-red crab crawling off the dish.

A friend of mine insists that in order to eat a crab with any comfort it is necessary to have at hand, besides the crab, a bowie-knife, a hammer, and a bucket of water.   Others, equally ignorant, insist that there is nothing to eat in a crab.   As a matter of fact, the opening of a crab can be made a pleasure, and there is really a great deal of delicious eating to be found.   To begin with, the outfit for crab-eating should consist of nut-picks, nut-crackers, finger-bowls, and napkins.   The big claws are easily broken open with the nut-crackers. The legs can be thrown away in times of plenty To get at the inside of a crab with neatness and despatch, turn up the under breastplate and break it off. Then the whole back can be lifted off, exposing a good deal of a yellow, greenish substance, which is the fat of the crab and its best relish. Having the crab divested of underplate and back-shell, break it in two, and the white meat will be readily extracted with a nut-pick. The muscles which operate the crab's claws and legs constitute the meat. A little practice will convince any one that crabs are not to be despised. Their flavor is incomparably finer than that of a lobster, while the scientific opening of a crab has all the charm of a surgical operation.

To those who contend that crabs are deadly poison, especially if eaten after dark, I can only say that I have experimented upon myself and upon a number of other people's children without unpleasant results. A crab (cooked) is one of the favorite playthings of babies in this neighborhood. It is said that milk and crabs, when taken together, raise a tempest inside of one. Again I may say that I

have experimented and escaped. The proba-
bility is, that people who eat crabs with vinegar
and other rich sauces ought not to drink milk
at the same time.

How to handle a crab is a subject better
taught by actual experience than by directions.
It is not so difficult a matter as most people
suppose, and the ladies who would no sooner
meet a crab than some terrible beast of prey—
say a mouse—are all wrong. I have known a
whole carful of people utterly demoralized by
a few poor timid little crabs. During the summer some friends who went crabbing with me
one day wanted to take a few fine specimens to
New York. I packed them carefully in a basket, with sea-weed below and on top, and over
all I tied a newspaper. It was dark when my
friend and his wife reached the railway. He
put the basket under the seat in the car and
went to sleep. Just as he was dreaming that
he had landed a crab as big as a porpoise, his
wife awoke him with a tragic whisper : "Harry,
the crabs are out—one has just walked over my
foot ! "

The situation was a critical one. The wet
sea-weed had weakened the paper covering of

the basket, and the crabs were coming forth in
a solemn procession ; by the looks of the basket, at least twenty must have gone—somewhere. My friend jammed a heavy shawl into
the basket over what remained, and awaited
developments in fear and trembling. They
were not long in coming. A shriek from a
lady at the other end of the car announced
that one crab had made his presence felt. All
was excitement in a moment. "She 's got
heart disease," said one old gentleman ; "stop
the train and get a doctor." "Catch it, catch
it, it 's under my seat, it 's bitten my foot!"
cried the poor woman. My friend had to do
something. "Ladies and gentlemen," he
shouted, "it 's all right. A few little crabs
that I had in a basket have escaped—that 's
all." That was all, was it ? Every woman in
the car jumped shrieking upon the seats, and
quiet was restored only when the last crab had
been kicked off the rear platform by the brake-
man.

If taken properly, the crab is the most harm-
less of dangerous beasts. Bear in mind that if
you take a crab firmly where the hind legs joins
his body, he cannot get at you with his nip-

pers ; also, that any quick motion disconcerts the crab for the moment, and you will be master of the situation. By a little experimenting you will find the exact place where a crab may safely be seized, and possibly some places where it is not safe. Rapid passes before the eyes of a crab appear to paralyze him. If, therefore, you quickly turn him over and over until you see an opportunity of seizing him by the hind leg close to the body, there is not one chance in five that the crab will get hold of you before you get hold of him. After all, suppose he does get a nip now and then ?—his revenge for ill-treatment is insignificant compared with what yours will be.

A T daylight all was bustle and preparation
for a fishing trip to Fire Island; one
would think from the excitement of the children that we went fishing but once a year instead of once a week, and that the prospect of
catching a fish was something altogether unusual. I do not remember a more perfect
morning. When Arthur and I started down
to the boat to see that all was ready, an iri-
descent mist hung over the bay, and the distant
highlands down toward Fire Island were tipped
with fire. The air was cool enough to make
one relish the idea that the sun would be warm
in a few hours, and there was enough promise
of a breeze to warrant a start as soon as breakfast had been disposed of. It was a pleasure
even to jump aboard the *Nelly* and get her
ready for her thirty-mile trip. The man who
does not love the water and a boat can scarcely
understand such joy as this; but to me and to

some people I know, a boat, and especially a sail-boat, is a never-failing source of pleasure. The fact that I have seen some pretty rough days in the *Nelly*, and that there have been times when I would not have wagered much upon my chances of getting her into port, seem rather to endear her to us; a boat that has stood a hundred gales, and has carried us thousands of miles, deserves something of gratitude in return. I cherish on the desk at which I now write a brass cleat from a little sail-boat I once owned; it serves as a paper-weight and as a reminder of scores of pleasure days. On one side of it is engraved the name of the boat, and on the other the date—"April-December, 1880." When the time came for selling her, I retained this memento of many an exciting sail, and, as my wife would add, of many a hairbreadth escape.

We hoisted the *Nelly's* sail to dry in the sun, and started back to breakfast. There were but few of the natives about the shore, but among those few I found my friend the Cap'n, who had been out to his nets, and had brought back a plentiful supply of " bunkers," which we could have as bait. These " bunkers " are the " bony.

fish," or the menhaden of the oil factories;
when our bay fishermen take them in their nets,
they are not thrown back, but are used as manure. As the Cap'n says, every "bunker"
represents a good-sized potato to him. For a
few cents we get a bucketful of them for bait.
It is six o'clock by the time we get back to the
house, to find the breakfast steaming on the
table. Half an hour later we are off to the
shore again, and before seven o'clock the *Nelly*
is bowling along westward at the rate of five
miles an hour. The village is still, to all in-
tents and purposes, asleep, although the sun
has begun to melt the mists, and the air has
lost the keen sharpness of an hour before. As
we glide along, all to the south of us, over towards the ocean, is one flood of golden light, with
the low ridge of the sand hills standing out in
shadow; above these lines of sand dunes the
morning sky is resplendent, and between us
and the beach the bay glitters with dancing
sunbeams. On the other side we have the
Long Island shore, with its hills and woods, its
farmhouses and hay-stacks. From our point of
view, about a mile out in the bay, we can see
the spires of half-a-dozen villages—Bellport,

Patchogue, Bayport, and Sayville among them. The prevalent idea to the effect that Long Island is a flat stretch of sand, is one of the first impressions to disappear when one gets out upon the water here. There are no mountains, to be sure, but we have respectable hills, and when seen from the water in certain lights they give a mountainous background to the country along the shore. To get the full effect of these Long Island hills as an imposing background, one has to sail from the Great South Bay down to Moriches on just such a morning as this. Starting from Patchogue at five or even at six o'clock, if the wind is fair, the entrance to the narrow strait at Smith's Point is reached before the mists rise, and one gets a view of Moriches, which has reminded more than one person I know of a miniature Swiss landscape. The little village seems to nestle at the foot of a range of mountains, more or less imposing, according to the power of the sun upon the mists. Sailing out of Patchogue, we could not imagine ourselves upon a Swiss lake, for the hills in the background were too far off to dominate the town ; moreover, the air was better than ever blew over Lake Geneva.

A fishing expedition to us who live nearly at the other end of the Great South Bay, means a •day's trip, as a rule, and as usual we get fairly off before we begin to take stock of the necessaries that have been left behind. It is a twelve-mile sail to the cinder-beds, as our fishing grounds are called, and as we are pretty sure to have to beat against the wind one way, it is called a thirty-mile sail there and back. There are five of us in the boat, not counting the children, and to two of our friends the trip is a novel one in every respect ; they had never been on the bay before, they had never seen a bluefish caught, and they had serious doubts as to whether a day on the water might not end in disaster. One of the ladies had braved the terrors of a thirty-mile sail, notwithstanding the fact that when she went last to Europe she was so sea-sick that " every thing came out of her except her immortal soul." Sailing on our bay is somewhat dangerous to sea-sick people, because it is so shallow that a breeze makes a sea in less time than it takes to tell it ; because the water is like a mill-pond in the morning is no promise that it may not be like the " raging main " by afternoon. Es-

pccially is this the case when the wind is from
the north.   I have recorded the results of a
"norther" often enough to feel certain as to
the day's weather on this water; when the
water is smooth, and the north breeze comes
in the morning like a zephyr, look out for a
squally gale by noon—one of the worst winds
we have for small boats.   It will blow in gusts
all day until the sun sinks, when it will die
away, and the day will end as it began.

As we sailed along I gave our friends some
details as to the life upon the Great South Bay,
its pleasures and its hardships, which may be
resumed in a few pages and may possibly interest people who know little about this part of
the coast and its sports. As between a life along
the coast and a life in the hills, I have found by
experience—my own and that of others—that
success depends largely upon temperament and
constitution.   There are people who cannot
stand salt air, much as they love it ; and I have
known earnest lovers of the sea and the coast
to suffer such agonies from throat and lung
troubles when living near the ocean, that no
amount of pleasure to be derived from water
sports could atone for these drawbacks. Every

man should make a certain number of experiments in determining what part of the world, within certain limits, is best suited to his needs and purposes. People are too prone to settle down meekly wherever the Fates cast them. There comes a time in life when almost every man can (perhaps by a little sacrifice) cut loose from money-making work of a routine character and take some sort of what I should call rational employment in the open air, whether it be fishing, gardening, or hunting. When such a time comes, why should not the man who determines upon so important a change, look over the whole field ? We have almost all conditions of climate and soil within a few days of us. I have known busy New-Yorkers to cut loose from the bank or the business desk, and adopt life down on the Cheseapeake Bay ; others have taken to raising oranges in Florida ; some of my own relatives have been for years engaged in vineyards and wine-making in California ; others, again, have taken to small fruits ; still others have embarked in sheep-raising in northern Connecticut, and made it pay. I myself, perhaps from timidity, have settled down within a few miles of New York, for

I find a good deal in favor of this sheet of water which constitutes our happy hunting-ground.

The common idea that the Long Island coast is simply one long stretch of sand, varied by occasional patches of green in the shape of salt meadows, called marshes by city visitors, may be true so far as concerns the country within forty miles of New York. But beyond that there is a decided change. There are actually hills to be seen here and there; not very high ones, but high enough to be called hills. Most persons who have noticed on the maps the words "Shinnecock Hills," wonder what kind of country this may be, for at the point where the Shinnecock reservation is situated, Long Island is but a mere neck of land, at one point not more than a few hundred rods wide. The Shinnecock Indians at one time occupied this part of the island, and their descendants are still to be found. Along the coast, starting from a point forty miles from New York, there are hills to be seen even far more imposing than the famous Shinnecock range, which is in reality merely a collection of sand dunes, scantily covered with grass upon which sheep are pastured. The central range of hills, or the back-bone of the island, is quite an imposing line when seen from the ocean, and even as viewed from the Great South Bay upon a misty morning it gives, as I have already said, quite an air of mountainous wilderness to the background. In former days, when the Great South Bay and Shinnecock Bay were deep enough to afford navigation for good-sized schooners, it is probable that all this region stretching between Islip on the west and East Hampton on the east, was the scene of much more animation the year round than at present. We who resort here for quiet are rather glad of the change. Old ocean has helped us. It has played such tricks with this coast that it seems to be only a matter of time when these bays will become wholly land-locked. Fifty years ago there was a large outlet to the ocean in the Great South Bay nearly opposite Patchogue, whereas now the boats have to go twenty miles farther down the bay to Fire Island inlet before they can go out into the ocean. Year after year, this Patchogue inlet grew narrower as each great storm washed up thousands of tons of sand. At last a great storm closed up the inlet, and it was only when the people went to work with shovels and carts that any communication between the bay and the ocean was maintained. For several years there was a day appointed, usually in the spring, when the farmers and fishermen within ten miles of Patchogue and Bellport were called upon to meet at the inlet and put in a day's work at digging. If the response to the call was a satisfactory one, the work of clearing out the channel to a depth of four or five feet right across the sand-bar took but a few hours; then, if there came up no great storm, such an inlet would last all summer, giving plenty of salt water to the bay. In the autumn the first great storms of winter filled up the inlet, and in the spring the work had to be done all over again. About twenty-five years ago it became evident that the ocean was a far better workman than the people of Patchogue, and was making it more and more difficult to keep up communication with the bay. As no vessels of any size could sail through this artificial ditch, the only use for it was to give salt water to the bay, and this benefited only the fishermen. So the farmers objected to working for this purpose, and the inlet was allowed to become so choked up that to-day it would cost thousands of dollars and months of labor to cut an opening at the place where half a century ago vessels sailed through.

In Shinnecock Bay, twenty-five miles farther along, exactly the same experience has been gone through within the last ten years; but the people of that neighborhood still keep up courage, and work at the inlet every spring, with the hope that nature will some day come to their assistance and restore the old channels. The canal, which the government is now cutting through the neck of land separating Shinnecock and Peconic bays, may create a current ocean-ward which will carry the sand out to sea. The reason for this greater activity upon the part of the Shinnecock people is that without communication with the ocean, Shinnecock Bay would soon become a fresh-water and a very unhealthy pond. Even now it is impossible to grow clams in Shinnecock Bay, once the best clamming spot along the coast, because the water is not salt enough, and if the canal does not help matters, the time is not far distant when, notwithstanding the yearly cleaning-out of the inlet, all fish and oysters will disappear.

At the upper end of the Great South Bay the effect of filling up the inlets communicating with the ocean has been felt chiefly by the fishermen. As there is no communication with the ocean, no sand of any consequence is thrown into the bay by winter storms. For the last twenty-five years the bottom of the Great South Bay has undergone no changes, and the soundings made by the government many years ago are still trustworthy. In the great storms of winter the spray of the ocean sometimes washes into the bay, rolling over the sand-bar, but the agitation of the water in the bay is not sufficient to cause the sand to shift. We have still a depth of from four to seven feet right up to the end of the bay, with long stretches of shallow flats, sometimes covered with grass, in which the ducks take shelter and feed in winter. These flats extend along the sand-bar from one to two miles into the bay, and any one who has sailed for a summer or two in the bay, learns pretty well how to keep clear of them by the .looks of the water. Along the main shore there is plenty of water for from two to three miles out from the shore, and this makes the bay a superb sailing-place for small boats. As for the fishing part, it has grown less and less, until to-day it is not what might be called a good fishing-ground, except within a few miles of Fire Island inlet, where the blue-fish still run in the right season. Perhaps the number of fishermen has had something to do with the scarcity of fish. The fame of Fire Island inlet has spread so far among lovers of bluefish that not a day passes from late June until late September when there cannot be found a fleet of from twenty to two hundred boats on the look-out for bluefish. The fishing industry of Babylon is entirely de-voted to taking out parties for bluefishing; the professional fisherman scarcely professes to fish at all. His duty is to keep his smack in order, to furnish bait and lines, and to be ready to pilot his patrons to the best place in the bay for a catch. Whether fish are caught or not, the fisherman gets his dollars, and finds it more profitable to take people fishing than to fish himself.

Oysters, of course, have remained one of the great resources of the Great South Bay. The fa-mous Blue Point, so named because of the blue tint of the weeds which formerly covered the

point, still remains the ideal spot of this region
for oyster-dredging, and when the summer vis-
itor runs away frightened by the first September storm, the oysterman takes off the fancy
trimmings of his boat, stores away the awn-
ings, camp chairs, and cushions, and prepares
for hard work.   In reality, the first two months
of oystering are what is to me the pleasantest
time of the year.   Once the September gales
have abated, the weather settles down into glorious days, and from early October until Christmas the Blue Point oysterer has an existence
which might be envied by any one fond of out-
door exercise.   On such days as these, the bay,
calm and peaceful, is given up to its rightful
owners.   The summer visitors have disappeared.   The smacks of the fishermen have
resumed their working appearance, the duck-
shooters have begun to sound the alarm along
the coast, and from sunrise to sunset, the air,
whether it comes from the ocean or from the
pine woods of the Long Island plains, is full of
a fragrance which cannot be found in the neighborhood of great cities.   People talk about the
sufferings of the oystermen, and we hear a
good deal about frozen hands, night work, and

perilous adventures. As a matter of fact, although I have followed the doings of the bay oystermen with considerable interest, I have found no evidences of exceptional hardship. It is cold work sometimes, but as compared to the work of a city car-driver it is sport. Although each oyster smack has a comfortable little cabin warmed by a stove, it is a common sight to see the oystermen eating their dinners in the sunlight on deck rather than keep to the cabin on a blustering December day. The worst that can be said of the life of the professional oysterman is that it does not pay, and even this may be called in question. The crew of a smack devoted to fishing in the bay, whether for bony fish for the oil factories, or for oysters, usually consists of two men and a boy ; the boy sails the boat, while the men attend to the nets or the dredges. The smack is worth from $600 to $1,200, according to size and appointment. I have known the profits of a season, which begins in June and ends when the bay freezes over in January, to be $2,500 for one smack. The fishing lasts till October, when the oystering begins. The boats are usually owned by the men who sail them, and

the boy who goes as sailor gets a percentage of
the catch, whether of fish or of oysters. One
young fellow who sailed in a Patchogue smack
last summer got $600 as the returns of his sum-
mer's work.

To-day, as the morning breeze dies away
about ten o'clock, leaving us in the middle of
the bay, two miles from land on either side, it
seems hard to believe that within a few weeks
the oystermen will be blowing on their fingers
and swinging their arms, and that the duck-
shooters will be ranging this very spot. The
water is so warm that it is still full of jelly-fish,
which the children catch with a scalp net as we
glide slowly along. Half an hour later the
breeze dies out entirely, and the boom swings
from one side to the other, the sail flapping
idly. No amount of whistling brings a breeze.
It is hot and still. The buzzing of an occasional fly and noises from the distant shore are
faintly heard; the barking of dogs and the
hammering of some carpenters are very distinct. As the little air moving comes from the
shore, we cannot hear the boom of the surf on
the other side of us. The cinder beds, our
fishing grounds, are still five miles away. By

watching the bottom, a few feet below us, we estimate that the boat is moving at the rate of one yard a minute, at which pace we shall get there some time next year. This is part of fisherman's luck, and the man who should feel resentment or show impatience in such circumstances has no business to go fishing on the Great South Bay, or anywhere else. We have books with us, we have hopes of a breeze to come and fish to be caught.

The true fisherman enjoys fishing whether he catches fish or not. The love of fishing is much akin to the love of gambling ; whether you win or lose there is pleasurable excitement about it. It is the hope of getting something for nothing, so to speak, and your true fisherman will sit upon the edge of a boat or the string-piece of a wharf all day, content to be there and meditate upon what he might have caught or may yet catch. The best fisherman I know are the old fellows who dangle their legs over the edge of the Paris quays waiting for goujons to bite—little fish half the size of a herring ; and the catch of a round half-dozen makes a red-letter day for the Seine fishermen. I remember a picture of two of these enthusiasts going home in a pelting rain with an empty creel between them. They have been out all day and are drenched to the skin. One says: "What a glorious sport this fishing is! What would life be without it?" "Yes, indeed," responds the other, "I shall never forget that nibble as long as I live!" This is the true spirit in which to fish.

I was pretty sure that upon so clear and cloudless a day there would be wind after the sun passed the meridian, and, sure enough, the breeze began to come clear and cold from the ocean before one o'clock. It was a good breeze to take us home, and so we determined to push on for a few miles more for the sake of trying the bluefish on the cinder beds. The enjoyment and refreshment of a cold wind after the sultry stagnation under a hot sun was reward enough for our previous discomfort, and the spirits of the party rose as the boom swung over to starboard and we started again for Fire Island, headed down the bay. Luncheon was got out, and we munched our sandwiches and prepared the tackle for fishing.

With the breeze a haze also spread over the horizon. South of us we had the Fire Island coast, which is here splendidly wooded with scrub oak and is dotted at long intervals with the summer-houses of people who care less for society than for nature. We were sailing within half a mile of the island. Back of us Patchogue was lost in the mist. The breeze grew fresher and fresher. The waves began to rise, and it was as lively sailing as any one could want when we reached the little fleet of fishing-boats lying on the cinder beds and cast out our anchor. We were late for the right tide, but as the crews of the other boats reported the fishing to be fair, we decided to try it. With such a breeze it would be less than a two hours' sail home, and it was not yet two o'clock. We should have time for an hour's fishing, for half an hour's run on shore in order to rest the children, and then we could make sail for home with a fresh wind at our stern for a ten miles' run.

The routine of our bluefishing I have described elsewhere. Fish are a secondary consideration. If we catch any, well and good ; if not, we have had a pretext for sailing thirty miles and idling away the day in the most profitable way imaginable. " L'Art de ne Rien

Faire " is after all one of the most difficult of
arts.   Nature and the animals flourish in idleness.   But man is supposed to deteriorate when
not engaged in producing things, or robbing his
neighbors in the *finesses* of trade.   If, because
of the vicious warp inherited from ancestors
who deified work for its own sake, we feel uncomfortable at the idea that we are sailing the
Great South Bay from morning till night with
no dollars in view, we may perhaps quiet our
utilitarian instincts by this pretext of fishing.
We are trying to obtain food for the family;
we may not have hoed any corn or dug any
potatoes, or written any articles which editors
may be willing to pay for, but we have tried to
provide food for the household, and our conscience is clear.   It may be said that this is but
a subterfuge, for if I had stayed at my desk
cudgelling my brains for ideas of merchantable
value, I should have earned enough money to
buy bluefish for the whole summer.   This may
be true, and yet I do not admit the force of
any such reasoning.   The mere ability to earn
enough money to keep one's family decently
sheltered, fed, and clothed is the most ordinary
ability in the world; the man who fails to do it

is either extremely unfortunate or uncommonly incompetent. He is the exception. We should aim to accomplish something more than what every one does. We should endeavor to eat our cake and keep it too. I am led to say all this in order to explain why it was that we did not give way to dejection when we discovered, after a throw or two of the lines, that the tide had turned and that there were no fish to be had. The other boats had begun to raise their anchors and were taking advantage of the fine southwesterly breeze to spread their wings for home. It was a question whether the wind would last until sundown or not. So the fishing was abandoned, and we sailed over to the wharfs near the oil-factories for a run on shore.

By the time that the last of the fishermen had made sail for home, we took up the tail of the procession. No more splendid breeze could be desired—straight from the southwest and without a flaw. With our centreboard up we cared not for flats—there was enough water for us,—and our course was laid straight for home. Every thing in the east was hazy, and it looked as if rain might be falling in the neighborhood of Montauk Point, for the sun was painting resplendent pictures upon the banks of clouds. Two hours later we swung around among our little Patchogue fleet and made fast to shore. The wind had gone down with the sun ; the bay was like a mirror, and we could hear the oars of people becalmed a mile from home.

AS I have already said elsewhere, my bees have contributed a few dollars a year to my income, and have given me a great many pounds of honey and no little amusement. Some five or six years ago a newspaper paragraph concerning the large amount of money to be made by raising bees and selling their honey caught my eye, and I had the curiosity to look up the only firm in this part of the country which at that time made a business of selling hives fitted out with bees. My investigation resulted in the purchase of a hive containing a swarm of pure Italian honey-bees warranted to do justice to their reputation as indefatigable workers, and to make my fortune if I looked after them with intelligence and perseverance. The people from whom I bought my first hive were full of information as to the vast amount of honey and, of course, profit I was to get from my investment; they said

nothing about a vast number of stings. According to the rosy picture which was drawn
of my future, I should merely have to buy my
hives and hire a convenient place in which to
store the honey as it was produced by the ton.
I was told that any neighborhood where vegetation throve was good for bees, and that an
able-bodied man could take care of two hundred hives with ease and live in comfort upon
the products of his little servants. The details
of the business were said to be easy to learn,
and its prosecution one long delight. In support of this story, I was presented with several
works by men who had kept bees and were
impelled from the enthusiasm which filled them
to tell the world how much money and joy
might be found in bee-keeping. One man
went so far as to give the actual amounts which
he had made in a few years, with fac-similes of
the checks he had received in payment for his
enormous shipments. According to his account, bee-keeping was the easiest, pleasantest,
and most profitable of all employments; all the
bee-keeper had to do was to take out the honey
from the hive and sell it to the misguided
people who keep no hives of their own. An-

other little book told of a bright young city
man who gave up the delights of the theatre
and base-ball matches to retire to the country
with a hive of bees; he emerged five years
later with something like a fortune made out
of honey.

The first supply was to be the only cost of
the enterprise beyond that of the hives in
which to place other swarms, and the little
boxes which are put in the hives to receive the
honey. I was assured that very few people
who took hold of the business gave it up
because of the stings they received, and that,
if I could take the opinion of all bee-keepers
upon the subject, I would find that it was
virtually a chorus of praise in honor of this
industry, which is almost literally as old as the
hills, and yet has been completely revolution-
ized, turned upside down, within the last
twenty years. For centuries people had gone
on allowing bees to do as they thought fit.
Twenty years ago an inventive genius discovered that the bees knew nothing about making
the most of their time, and were living a life of
riotous idleness.

It is some five years since, thus induced to

consider the bee business as something which offered me exactly what I wanted—a life of ease, with nothing to do and plenty of money, —I paid $15 for my hive stocked with bees, $1 for a veil to put over my head, $2 for a pair of rubber gloves, and several dollars more for various implements to be used, as I found out afterwards, in fighting the infuriated insects. My bill for the original outfit was $20 and some cents, according to the accounts of the business, which I have kept with great care, and which are now before me. During these five years I have had an experience worth all the money paid out, and as there may be some other people anxious for a life of ease and plenty of money, my experience may not be without interest and profit to them. Seriously, I have not had a bad time of it, and for the number of hours and the amount of money which I have devoted to my bees, I am inclined to congratulate myself over the result, and to advise others to at least make the experiment of keeping a few hives. I have never thought of honey-making as any thing but the amusement of idle hours in the country, and I first gave time and thought to bee-raising very much as I might to chicken-raising or any other hobby of the city man who has only a few hours in the country which he does not devote to sleep.

My first hive was bought when I was living in the Orange Mountains of New Jersey, about twenty miles from New York. It arrived by express, the top of the hive covered with wire-cloth, through which the bees peered rather curiously but not at all viciously. The directions were to take off the wire-cloth as carefully as possible, and put on a large wooden cover. As the construction of a modern beehive is radically different from that of the old-fashioned straw one, I may as well say a few words about it. The essential part of a modern hive consists of a wooden box eighteen inches wide, two feet long, and about fourteen inches deep. This box contains from eight to ten "frames," which are filled up with a sheet of comb of the average thickness. These sheets of comb, sometimes partly filled with honey by the bees, hang side by side in the hive, and usually occupy the whole of the box. It is possible to lift out any one of the frames and see exactly what is going on upon the sheet of comb it contains. The same sheet may be partly given up to honey, or may contain young bees in the various stages of growth from the egg to the live bee. In the spring there is usually very little honey left in the hive, the bees having eaten it all during the winter, and filled up the empty cells with eggs, fast becoming bees. The frames of the hives are not often disturbed by the beginner in bee-hiving, since the bees are apt to resent this investigation into their private apartments. Above the box containing the frames comes a cover, which is sufficiently high to allow a number of honey-boxes to be placed right on top of the frames. These honey-boxes are easily contained in a large case, which enables them all to be put on or lifted off together. In this case there are from twenty to thirty boxes to be filled by the bees. In some hives boxes for honey are also placed in the lower part of the hive along the outside walls, when the bees will often fill them in preference to going up into the cover of the hives.

In the old-fashioned hives it was necessary to kill the bees by suffocating them with sulphur smoke before the honey could be cut out of the hive. In the new hives, if I may so call the

hives which date from twenty years ago, the
bees are never much disturbed when honey is
taken out of the hive ; the idea of killing bees
in order to get honey would now be considered
atrocious barbarism. The modern method of
taking the honey-boxes out of the hives is simply to drive the bees from the boxes down to
their own frames by the use of the smoke of
rags, when the boxes may be lifted off without
injuring the bees. About five hundred patents
have been taken out within the last twenty
years for improved beehives, and the farmers
in some parts of the country have been so
annoyed by the claims of people who pretend
to own patent rights upon hives which they
had purchased, that the rapacity of these hive
inventors has driven many of them out of the
business. The moment a man bought what
seemed to be a sensible and cheap hive, he was
called upon to pay royalties to some one who
claimed the patent. The number of different
hives, each type having its champions, is a very
large one, and almost every well-known bee-
keeper has left a hive of his own devising which
is expected to do something that other hives
will not do. It has been found by long experi-

ence that bees are very accommodating insects, and will adapt themselves to almost any variety of home, provided it is sufficiently dark and secure from the attacks of animals.

My first year's experience consisted in opening the hives every day or two, after suffocating all the bees with five times the necessary amount of smoke, and studying what was going on inside. This effectually prevented the bees from making any honey, but it gave me some insight into their habits, and a very perfect knowledge of the treatment of stings. As to honey, the first year was only a partial success. The very day after the beehive arrived and had been put in place, I put over the frames every honey-box that came with the hive, and watched for the result. In one of my books it is recorded that a swarm of bees will sometimes bring in as much as twenty pounds of honey in one day; my bees had evidently never read this book. I could not find that they brought in an ounce, unless for their own use. After some weeks of anxious watching and disappointment, I consulted a neighbor, who knew somebody else whose brother had once had a beehive, and in the end I discovered that an old farmer ten

miles off had some bees, and actually got some
honey from them every year. I went to see
him, and found out that in that part of Jersey,
at least, bees do very little in the way of honey-
making from the end of June until the end
of August; moreover, that if I want to get
them to make honey in the little boxes which
are sold by the grocers, I should have to encourage them by placing in each box a little
sheet of wax marked with the comb indenta-
tions. These wax " starters " are the invention
of a German bee-keeper. I also learned that,
in order to get the bees to do their whole duty,
a modern device, likewise the invention of a
German, known as an " extractor," would be
necessary.

The extractor is simply a tin barrel containing a frame which can be made to whirl around
upon a central pivot. Into this frame the hive
combs, when they contain honey, are placed,
and made to revolve so rapidly that the honey
is forced out of the cone by centrifugal action
and trickles down to the bottom of the extract-
or. Before bees begin to store honey in the
little boxes in the top of the hive, they first fill
up such parts of the large frames as are not

used by them for rearing young; and the motion of the extractor is so regulated that the eggs and young bees are not thrown out with the honey. The comb having been emptied of the honey, the frame is replaced in the hive, and the bees, finding their stores gone and fearing starvation, will go to work again with the energy of despair. Some bee-keepers use their bees entirely for producing this extracted honey, and never make any box-honey, as the honey in the comb is called. The sale of extracted honey, put up in bottles, is naturally larger than that of box-honey, as it can be kept in better order and for a longer time; but its price is less by several cents a pound, and the temptation to adulterate it with sugar and water has given it a bad reputation in some communities. As yet no one has found a method of making artificial comb and filling it with artificial honey. A dealer in honey said to me one day: " These rascals who adulterate honey with glucose are ruining our business in extracted honey. Fortunately, they cannot imitate comb-honey. It has been tried, but does not succeed; I would give $10,000 to find a good method of doing it." So much for business virtue. The only way in which adulteration comes into play with comb-honey is in the practice of feeding the bees upon glucose or maple-sugar and water, which mixture they, of course, store up in the boxes and "cap" over in the usual way, as if it was genuine honey from flowers.

The internal economy of a beehive, with its thousands of workers, its drones, and its one queen, has been described so often in print that I need not waste space upon it. A good beehive, well filled, contains about 25,000 bees. My first beehive had about 5,000 when it came to me, but reached the maximum before the end of the autumn. When the queen lays eggs, she does so at the rate of several hundred a day, and in less than three weeks the bees from these eggs are flying around. Much has been said of late as to the superiority of the Italian bee, which carries three yellow bands upon its body, over the native black bee, and as high as $50 have been paid for a good Italian queen. Means have been devised of so packing queens that they often come from Europe by mail, and are sent all over the country in the same way. The average price for a good queen is at present one dollar. At the end of my first summer's experience in the bee business, and after allowing my bees to take care of themselves for the six weeks from the middle of September to the end of October, I found that I had twelve pounds of honey stored up in boxes, and that the nine frames of the lower part of the hive were completely full of honey and weighed eight pounds apiece. I took out three of the frames which were filled and left in six for the winter, thus giving the bees nearly fifty pounds of honey to live upon. The preparation for winter in Jersey is simply to take off the top and side boxes, filling up the void with sawdust; I left the hive out-of-doors, and I have followed the same plan in Connecticut with success. In northern New England and in the northwestern States, where the thermometer often falls below zero, it is customary to winter the hives in cellars.

After a pretty severe winter I discovered in the first sunshiny days of March that my bees were coming out of the hive freely, and taking a warm day for investigation, I lifted out a frame to find it full of " brood," as the bees not yet out of the cell are called. As the spring

advanced the hive became more and more
lively, and when the willows blossomed the
noise of my bees could be heard fifty feet
away; apparently I had twice as many bees as
in the autumn, and I looked forward to a tremendous crop of honey. Authorities upon
the bee business say that the average product
of a good hive ought to be 60 pounds of
honey a year. Some bee-keepers boast of
having obtained 100 pounds, and the farmer
who still keeps bees in a common wooden box,
provided with no movable frames, is satisfied
with 25 or 30 pounds. May came, and I filled my
hives with boxes fitted out with wax "starters."
The hive appeared to be crowded with bees, so
much so that early in May a tremendous swarm
came out one day, and after hanging to a cedar
tree for some hours, went off to find new
quarters; I was away in the city and lost it.
Swarming is nothing more or less than a sign
that the hive is too small for the family. The
queen goes off with a certain number of the
bees to find a new home, but not without leaving things in such a state that a new queen
will be hatched out in a few days. Within ten
days of the loss of my first swarm, another one

appeared on a Sunday, and I found it without difficulty hanging to a small cedar tree. I put the cover on an old soap-box, and bored two or three holes in one side of the box with an auger. Then I put it on the ground near my first hive, carefully cut off the small limb upon which my swarm had clustered, and laid the black mass down in front of the soap-box, within an inch or two of the auger holes. The bees made a straight line for these openings, tumbling over one another in their anxiety to get in. In half an hour the last one entered. The next day I bought an empty hive in town. Upon opening my soap-box to get the bees into the new hive, which I did within forty-eight hours, I found that they had already begun making comb and the queen had begun to lay eggs. I made the transfer without difficulty. During this second year my two hives gave me between them forty-seven pounds of honey in boxes, and thirty-two pounds of honey which I cut from the frames. I found that the best honey season in that part of the country was not in the spring, but in the late autumn, the golden-rod affording most of the supply. At the close of the second summer I prepared the bees as usual and left them out in the snow for the winter.

In May following I increased my number of hives to four by taking out half of the bees in each of my two hives and putting them into new hives. The process is too complicated for description here; every bee-book gives a detailed account of how to do it. I succeeded perfectly. From my two old hives came a swarm apiece, both of which I succeeded in catching. This gave me six hives. The third year resulted in a harvest of 120 pounds in boxes and 90 pounds in the frames. The result was not so good as it might have been had I watched the hives carefully enough to determine exactly when the frames ought to have been emptied of their contents by the use of an extractor. I have never taken the trouble to get an extractor at all, preferring to work entirely for box-honey. Also, I did not take out my boxes as fast as they were filled, and this had something to do with the work of the bees, who do their best when starvation threatens them. For the fourth year, inasmuch as six hives were simply flooding me and my neighbors with honey, I neglected to hive the swarms at all, and simply let them go, knowing that more honey would mean a serious amount of time taken in looking after the hives and in selling the honey. The last year has given me no less than 280 pounds of honey in boxes and 160 pounds in the frames. Half of this honey has been sold at an average price of 14 cents a pound, which is about two thirds of the price obtained for it by the local grocer to whom I sold it.

To sum up the results of my experiments in bee-culture, I have six hives completely filled with bees and ready for the winter, which have cost me in all $46, including the original outlay. During the five years I have spent exactly 80 cents in food for the bees; when the spring is very late, they sometimes require to be helped along with a little candy. I estimate the value of my plant at $100, and my honey which remains for the winter's consumption at $30. The time necessary to look after and take care of 6 hives is certainly not more than three hours a week, and the number of stings received depends upon the caution and skill of the bee-keeper. I have found that it is not necessary to be stung at all, and that even when a few bees do manage to sting, it is not a very serious matter. Any man who wants a most interesting hobby can find no end of interest and some honey by getting a beehive and putting it on the roof, even if he lives in the city. Some years ago one of our downtown janitors, who kept a small apiary on the top of a big office building, had to give it up because a neighboring candy-shop on Broadway complained of the clouds of bees which the candy attracted. With judicious management one hive ought to give enough honey for a family, and to require almost no attention. Bees will fly four miles in search of honey, so that our New York city bees get most of their supplies in Jersey or over on Long Island. At one time a few years ago California honey seemed about to drive our Eastern bees out of the business. Since then, however, there has been a reaction, and our honey is preferred for its flavor, and higher prices are paid for it. One bee-keeper of Cherry Valley, New York, exports yearly to England $25,000 worth of honey raised by his own bees. I am now about to move my bees down to my Long Island home, having found that there are thriving apiaries in the neighborhood and plenty of buckwheat and golden-rod for their sustenance. If I cannot get several hundred pounds of honey every year to offset my grocery bill I shall be disappointed.

I AM sorry for the man who cannot get pleasure out of a wood fire. One of the promising signs of the times, according to my view, is the reappearance of the open hearth in most of our modern country-houses. If the æsthetic movement in house-building leaves us no other memento of its passage than the big open hearth and the andirons of our forefathers, we can afford to be thankful, for its sins are as nothing as compared to this blessing. Twenty years ago, one could find all over the country noble old houses in which the big fireplace had been bricked up in order to substitute a grate for coal, or, what is worse, a pipe-hole for a stove. With the better sentiment of the last few years, the fortunate people who own such houses have had the bricks torn down and the old andirons rescued from the attic. At my own fireside I have a pair of andirons that have been in use in the family for more than a hun-

dred and fifty years, and it is no small pleasure
to dream of the people, long since dead and
gone, who have watched the flames reflected in
those burnished brass relics of the olden time.
The man who has not learned to love a log fire
has missed one of the comforts of life ; it is the
love of a fire which has kept me from moving
to Florida or some country where vegetation
and gardens flourish the year round.   Fond as
I am of working among growing things, and
eagerly as I look forward year after year to the
first dandelion, I cannot bear the idea of losing
my noble blaze and the peculiar odor which a
log fire, especially of pine wood, gives to a room
when the winter blast outside sends an occasional whiff of smoke and flame down the chimney.   Along with the petty miseries of life in
large cities I should be inclined to place the absence of a wood fire, for even if there is a big
fireplace, which is not always the case in a city
house of the ordinary type, wood is too dear to
allow of its use as I understand it.   I want a fire
of logs a foot through and four feet long, which
burns from morning till late at night, which
throws out light enough to do without lamps
until the dinner-bell rings, and I am sure that

the children who grow up with the remembrance of that fire-light hour before their bed-time will be the better for it. It will inculcate in them a love of something healthy, spiritually and physically. Thoreau says: " Dead trees love the fire."

Of all the woods that we burn upon our big hearth in winter, the balsam pine knots are the most precious, because they send out an aromatic odor through the room somewhat akin to that of sandal-wood. Often, when the gale does not send us a whiff of smoke backing down the chimney, I take a pine knot out of the fire with the tongs and wave it through the room for the sake of getting that peculiar scent which has always seemed full of medicinal properties. In order to get pine knots of the kind I want, we make two or three trips every summer to a wooded headland within six miles of us, where for a trifle the owner has given me the privilege of cutting down a lot of old pines that are fit for nothing but firewood or fence posts. These firewood expeditions are hailed with delight by the children, because each one constitutes a sort of picnic for them. Yesterday was one of our firewood days, and we got

off by a glorious morning soon after seven
o'clock, taking, of course, all the children and a
friend with us. As we marched down to the
boat, our axes, fishing-poles, and oars over our
shoulders, we met the first stage starting from
our little hotel for the railroad station, full of
unfortunate business men bound to New York
for another week's heat, worry, fatigue, and
money. I suppose that every one of them
hoped to make at least one hundred dollars by
the week's work, for life is expensive when one
has a large family and boards at the country
inn. That would be about fifteen dollars a day.
I was going to earn enough firewood, or rather
enough pine knots, to give a balsamic scent to
our fires for half the winter. Probably I could
have hired a man to go and do the work for me
and bring back more wood than I should require, all for three or four dollars. If money is
the object of life, then my conscience ought to
prick me to the quick as we nod good-bye to
the money-makers and keep on down to the
bay. There is but little breeze stirring, scarcely
enough to send us along. Nevertheless, up
goes the sail, the children throwing aboard
their baskets and bags containing the lunch-

eon, and we cast off prepared for a good day's outing.

It sometimes occurs to me whether there may not be such a thing as the cultivation of idleness—whether the love of idleness does not grow by idleness. Many people have told me that the normal man needs to work in order to be healthy and happy, and by work they mean money-making of some kind. This giving a whole day to going after a quarter of a cord of pine knots would be looked upon as a peculiarly vicious idleness because of the specious attempt to dissimulate. I remember many years ago, when quite a young man, that chance threw me out of business for several months, and as it happened I employed most of my time in stripping a superb orchard of its apples and barreling them for sale in the city. I forget exactly what the venture netted me in money. The apples were going to waste and I invested the necessary money in empty barrels and freight charges. The work, I did myself, beginning before breakfast and stopping when it grew too dark to tell a good apple from a bad one. Then I went back to routine work at my own profession. But in after years the memory of that

apple-picking became a delight. I often spoke
of it to friends, only to be told that no one but
the laziest of men would think of wasting
months in an apple orchard. Perhaps as a
business investment, such work might pay the
wages of a day laborer, but it was unworthy of
a man who could earn ten or twenty dollars a
day by writing newspaper articles or trading in
lead pipe or leather. Moreover, I was assured
that had I kept on for a few months longer at
such work, it would have filled me with profound discontent and a wild desire to get back
to the city at any cost. I was assured that for
any man above the rustic lout, the country and
all its occupations would be intolerable except
as a recreation for a few weeks of the year,
unless there was plenty of money wherewith to
live a life of absolute idleness and watch others
work. It has always been taken for granted by
these good friends of mine that this is so self-
evident as to require no argument. The man
who wants to earn bread and butter for his
family must work in the city. Yet all these
years, I have retained a sneaking fondness for
the belief that years of work in an apple orchard
might not result disastrously for me or mine.

I recall the fact that during those three months
I was never better in health, that I never took
greater pleasure in my books and papers, that I
never looked upon life with more satisfaction.
And this accidental taste of country life at a
profit of a dollar or two a day, a small sum as
compared to my city earnings, had great influence in my determination to cut loose from
the city for a large part of the year.

To come back to the Great South Bay, it was
as smooth as a mill-pond, as we made sail for
our headland, looming up cool and shady to
the eastward. The water was so clear beneath
us that each patch of oysters could be dis-
tinguished on the bottom. Our friend M.,
whom we had along with us, and to whom I
sang the praises of a pine-knot fire, suggested
that if every one took to wood fires and burned
up a dozen cords of wood in the winter, as
we did, wood would become exorbitantly dear,
and none but millionaires would be able to
afford it. It is said that it takes the wood of
five square miles every year to furnish matches
for the world, the daily consumption in this
country reaching ten matches per head for

every man, woman, and child. And about once
a year the papers contain articles warning the
people that our forests are disappearing, never
to grow again. This sort of talk is rather lost
upon any one who lives down on Long Island
anywhere beyond. Babylon, for here there are
tracts of country where one can walk for miles
and miles without meeting a soul or seeing
a house, and yet covered with a growth of
excellent firewood, untouched almost from
generation to generation. Yet we are within seventy-five miles of the greatest city on
the continent. If New York City should ever
take to wood fires, Long Island can grow
wood just as well as cabbages. Even now,
when our Long Island woods have been shame-
fully neglected for generations, no one ever
thinking of replanting a forest that has been
cut down or burned up, good firewood, of
pine or oak, can be bought for three dollars a
cord, cut and delivered. A cord of wood will
give a roaring blaze every night for a month.
If you cut the wood yourself, as I do, you can
have it almost for nothing. There may come
a time when wood will become scarce in this
neighborhood, but it will not be in my day or

in the day of the children whom I am teaching to look upon a blazing hearth as an essential feature of home. By that time, man will probably get his heat from stored-up sunlight, or from electricity furnished by the rush of the tides or the sweep of the winds.

As we have a good hour's sail before us, one of the party reads out Thoreau's chapter on firewood, a wonderful study which rather dwarfs all attempts to say much upon the same subject. This is what I call a happiness beyond the making of any number of dollars. Here we are in our staunch, safe boat, gliding along with just enough sea breeze to take us to that haven where we would be, my wife and children finding health and spirits in it, a few books and magazines, and the prospect of several hours of hard, healthy work in the woods before we make sail for home as the sun goes down. The boom of the surf is the only sound that comes to us as we reach the middle of the bay and head straight for the little half-rotten dock which is all that is left of some improvements made years ago by a company of speculators who expected to establish a summer resort at the point we are steering for. Away

to the north of us a puff of steam or smoke
shows where the locomotive is dragging those
poor wretches off to their daily treadmill.
How very far away all such life seems. If it
were not for the daily newspapers, I should
almost forget that there were so many miserable beings grinding out their few years of
existence with so utter a disregard of the essential facts in the case. That puff of smoke
is the last reminder of civilization that we shall
have during the day before we sight our village
again. As the last line of Thoreau's chapter is
read, the boat swings round into the breeze and
Arthur jumps ashore and makes us fast, while
we gather up our implements of work. The
shore here presents a picture not unusual at
this part of the bay. For three or four hundred feet from the water there is a meadow
filled with low bushes and blackberry vines of
the creeping type. Then comes a rise in the
ground, and a plateau stretches away to the
north, covered with a heavy growth of trees.
The spot is a superb one for a big hotel or a
colony of cottages, and undoubtedly it would
long ago have been used for this purpose but
for the distance from the railroad; it is a five-

mile drive to the nearest railway station, and that would be a fatal waste of time to any business man. One of the reasons given for the success of the big hotel at Babylon is that it stands so near the railroad that the New Yorker can step from his train to the piazza of the hotel.

The shore presents this morning a beautiful picture of absolute calm. At nine o'clock nothing is heard as we stand on the little wharf and survey the scene but the distant boom of the surf to the south of us on the other side of the sand-bar, and the singing of the birds in the woods around us. The bay sleeps quietly in the sunlight, and the whole Long Island coast is in brilliant relief, with its hills in the background, just beginning to show the first tints of autumn. Our miniature forest is but a five minutes' stroll up to the headland, and the children begin an attack on the last of the blackberries as we go along. Upon reaching our grove I spied my old friend the Cap'n coming along the shore in his cat-boat from a visit to some distant eel-pots, and with the conviction that he may have something worth buying besides eels, I go down to the shore

and hail him. I stand high in the Cap'n's consideration just now—that is, as high as any
land lubber can ever expect to stand, for I have
placed at the side of my writing-desk one of
his eel-pots which I use as a scrap-basket. I
got the Cap'n to make it for half a dollar, and
as I couldn't quite make him understand for
exactly what purpose I wanted it, as a waste-
basket is something he had never heard of, he
made me a perfect eel-pot, and having put it in
place I called him in and showed him how
admirably its served its purpose. It was nauti-
cal, ichthyological, and harmonizes with the
room full of nets, poles, and guns. The Cap'n
was so much pleased with the sight of his eel-
pot half full of the waste from my desk that I
can scarcely get him to accept pay for bait, and
some day I think that he will show me a few of
the places in the bay where weak-fish are really
caught, instead of many places where they are
not, as is the custom with professional fishermen. Sure enough, the Cap'n has a bushel of
clams in his boat which he is taking over to the
beach for a friend, and it is not hard to divert
the store to our own purposes. The children
come down to the shore and I pull the basket

up the bank under the shade of some pines,
while they begin to collect firewood enough for
a clambake at dinner-time. If we cannot get
clams at our end of the bay, the water being
too fresh so far from an ocean inlet, we can at
least have them brought from fifteen to twenty
miles farther down, and then they can be
thrown into the water, where they will live for
months, to be taken up whenever wanted.

The real work of the day then began. While
the ladies sewed and read in the shade, and
the children picked late blackberries, we sturdy
laborers undertook to cut down half-a-dozen
small pines and saw their gnarled limbs into
suitable pieces for the fire. It was hot work,
and it made it hotter to think of the blaze
that we were preparing for. To quote Thoreau again, he used to say that he got more
warmth out of cutting his firewood than out
of its blaze, and his conscience was never quite
easy as to the return he made for the blessings
of a log fire. He used to say that though he had
paid money to the owner of that wood, he was
never quite sure that the debt had been wholly
discharged. In two hours we had done enough
of our work to see that with a little sawing

after dinner there would be sufficient to load up the boat, and then after a short rest we began to prepare for dinner. Whoever wants to know what clams are worth, must cook them on the shore, and with drift-wood picked up for the purpose. I have tried a clam-bake in our garden, I have tried it on the kitchen stove, but whether the difference is in the clams or in our appetites, the result is never the same. It is the easiest thing in the world to bake clams to perfection, if a few simple rules are observed. Sweep a flat space upon the sand, and lay upon it the sort of griddle made for the purpose, which can be found all over Long Island. The clams are held upright in this griddle, which holds at least one hundred, and sometimes more. Right on top of the clams build a loose fire of the drift-wood, and after it has blazed well for five minutes, and the clams begin to hiss violently, half smother it with wet sea-weed; a moment after, one or two clams may be tested. Pick one out with a pair of tongs and throw it up in the air, letting it come down upon any hard surface, a board, or a stone. If it flies open, all is well, and the feast may begin; if not, the clams are not quite done. When all is ready, shovel them into a large tin pan. We always keep the implements for a clam-bake in one of the lockers of the boat, for scores of times every summer we find that we can have a clam-bake when we least expected it, just as it happened this morning. Two hundred clams disappeared among seven of us, almost sooner than it takes to tell the tale, and back we went to our work.

As I shouldered my axe again I could not help one more thought of the miserable toilers in town. Was I stealing a living? If so, the old adage regarding stolen sweets once more proved true. The children are set at work carrying the wood down to the shore ready to be put on board, and even the youngest, a sturdy damsel of not quite four, shouts with indignation if any one proposes to help her along with her load. It is not four o'clock when we have enough wood to fill up the sail-boat, and we have to put some of it on deck. It has turned out to be a pretty hot day, and as there is enough breeze to take us home in less than an hour, we decide for a surf-bath, and the *Nellie's* prow is turned over to the beach, a mile off. I suppose that with some people the daily surf-bath from June till October might become so much a matter of course as to lose half its delights. As with country life, so it is with the surf, so far as I am concerned. It is always the keenest of pleasures and never more so than after a good day's hard physical work. By five o'clock we make sail for home, and for an hour we have before us a more splendid painting than was ever made by man. Here, on the Great South Bay, we seem to be particularly favored in the matter of sunsets, for certainly more than half our days end with one of these color displays as changing as it is indescribable. We have grown so used to these wonderful pictures that adjectives and superlatives have long ago been used up; some one points now and then to a particularly exquisite blending of gold and silver, and the rest of the party nod in silence. By the time we reach our harbor, the sun has gone down with the breeze, and we drift slowly into the little slip. The village is at supper, and my friend, the Cap'n, who stands on the dock, is the only one to greet us. He peers curiously at the wood, and seems

doubtful when I tell him that it is to burn.
For the Cap'n also has his ideas about queer
people who waste a whole day and sail ten
miles to get a lot of pine knots that any " nig-
ger" would have delivered for a two-dollar bill.
The Cap'n's notion of *otium cum dignitate* is
probably an unfailing supply of tobacco, and an
endless conference around the village store stove
upon the affairs of the neighborhood and the
nation. I told him once that I should think
he would enjoy making eel-pots, for the work
has a certain fascination about it—this weaving
together of strong, supple twigs of oak, the
converting of an old log into hundreds of pots
that will do duty for years. Every day the
Cap'n can feel that he has produced something
of value, which is more than a great many
more pretentious people I know of can say.
Down comes the sail, and while the boys tie it
up and make the ropes ship-shape for the night,
we gather up our traps and start for the house,
leaving the Cap'n deep in thought, as he
squints first at the horizon and then at our
little pile of logs. Even twelve hours of open
air have not quite satisfied me, and were it not
for several letters to write and a good many

proof-sheets to read, I should like to join the Cap'n in a tour of his eel-pots. There is no wind, so that the bay reflects every star as it peeps out, and away down in the southwest we catch a gleam from the Fire Island light.

IT has often been urged that such a scheme as
mine would be all very well for a man with
even a small income, say sufficient to insure him
and his family against starvation at any time,
and to give him the few luxuries which with
most people of refinement have become almost
necessary. For instance, even an income of
five hundred dollars a year might warrant a
person of very simple tastes in making such an
experiment as I have outlined; such a sum
would, at least, provide oatmeal and milk, bread
and coffee. It would be largely a return to
first principles in household economy, but there
are people who would not grumble could they
exchange a life of intellectual plenty even at
this cost of superfluities. So modest a sum
as five hundred dollars a year, if used with skill,
might provide a glimpse of such dissipation as
an occasional theatre, or a strain of music in

the depth of winter, the only time when the real countryman would have the time to leave his home, or the inclination to do so. The rest of the year would be pretty fully taken up. In my own case, it happens that unlike most men who have to look to the earnings of the year for bread and butter, I can throw all city work overboard when the spring opens, and not set foot in town before the snow flies. To most men, and to all business men, such an arrangement is impossible; the merchant cannot interrupt his work for so long a time with any certainty that he will be able to pick it up again; the clerk in a shop or a factory must be at his post all the year around, or not at all; the lawyer has to "keep track" of his clients' affairs, or he would soon find himself without clients. The world's machinery cannot stop, and the engineers must be at their posts. There are very few occupations outside of certain departments of journalism which can be taken up and thrown down at will. The merchant, the clerk, the lawyer, the doctor, must remain at their posts pretty much the year around, and this rule obtains all the more strictly with subordinates.

Therefore the problem becomes in the case of ninety-nine men out of a hundred : Either to give up one or the other. I have listened to scores of persons to whom I have submitted this problem, who are very certain that no man, especially if bred in a large city, would consent to forsake the pleasures of the town for the quiet of the country. I took the trouble once to find out, as nearly as possible, exactly what the average business man means by the word "pleasure." It seems that in the opinion of the typical young man of business, pleasure means going to the theatre once or twice a week, meeting large numbers of other young men and young women in the shops, or in the streets, or in their homes, or at church. The essence of this pleasure is the crowd,— largely of inane people characterized by unrest, hurry, or idle curiosity. This same love of the crowd characterizes many strata of society in cities, and the disease seems to thrive by what it feeds upon. As an illustration, take the history of the efforts made by one of our charitable societies to induce some of the very poorest inhabitants of our most squalid neighborhoods to get into the country. For nearly twenty years the district lying between the Bowery and the East River in New York City has been crowded with very poor people, who make a business of sewing upon ready-made clothing. They are largely Polish Jews of small intelligence, and apparently no instinct beyond self-preservation.   They live, or rather herd, together in vile holes, for which they pay exorbitant rents, and their life is one long struggle and incessant work.   According to credible reports, work begins soon after daybreak and lasts far into night, when the poor wretches sink down exhausted upon the piles of clothing which they are making for the cheap shops of the country.   Whole families live and die in this wretchedness, the children knowing no childhood, as we understand it, and old age being out of the question in this atmosphere of foul air and incessant toil.   It is not the work of healthy people, but a nervous strain to accomplish two days' work in one.   In many visits which I have made to such homes, I have invariably noticed that the workers seldom look up, and then only for a hurried glance—time is too precious.   Well, the society in question attempted to solve the problem before them.

Here were thousands and thousands of people who never knew what rest or recreation really meant, whose children had never seen a green field, or had had a real play in good air, whose lives were apparently hopeless. Ask some of the most intelligent of these slaves of the needle why they cannot move out into the suburbs where they could get nice little cottages for less money than they pay in their horrible quarters in the tenement districts, and the answer is always that they cannot spare the time needed to go back and forth with the bundles of clothing upon which the family labors. In New York such errands require but a few moments; in the country they would take up time and money for car fares.

The society resolved to do away with that trouble by paying for the expressage of clothing to and from the city for people who might like to move away, and a quiet spot was found out on Long Island where a dozen little houses were made ready for the first colony of these people. When it came to actually leaving New York there was some trouble in inducing a dozen families to go, but by collecting people with many children and making the rents of the cottages almost nominal, a dozen families were found to make the experiment. In less than a year and a half the scheme was abandoned. At no time were the cottages all occupied after the first month, and it required great inducements to prevail upon the tenants to remain more than a quarter. The reasons given by them for returning to New York were, in all cases, the same: the women of the family were lonely—they missed the society of the tenements. They missed the life of the streets, the drunken brawls, the yells and screams, the dirt, the noise, the heat, the foul air, and language of the slums. The children may have enjoyed the country, but their elders wanted society. Going higher in the social scale, it seems to be very much the same story. People with not much to think about cannot get on without the crowd, no matter what kind of a crowd. I am convinced that this is a far more potent factor in keeping people in great cities and attracting them than the prospect of better clothes and whiter hands which the shop offers to the young man from the farm. Therefore in order to wean city people, who ought not to live in the city, away from improper environment it is necessary to influence them in some other way than the offer of purely physical or economical advantages. Probably but very little can be done in this field except through the children, and the value of the work accomplished by the Children's Aid Society in sending out waifs picked out from the streets to green fields and pastures new in the far West, cannot be overestimated. With the average young man or young woman, who finds ample enjoyment in the gossip of the shops and is inclined to pity any one condemned to country life, I am inclined to think that the case is almost equally hopeless. The man who takes nothing into the country with him, intellectually speaking, ought not to go there; he will be lonely. I was strongly impressed with this phase of the matter when I made some visits among the cheap shops which line Grand Street, east of the Bowery. There are large shops here, employing hundreds of clerks of both sexes. Work begins early and lasts until seven or eight o'clock in the evening. In many of the shops it is so dark that gas or electric lights have to be used at mid-day. The neighborhood is alive with people of the lower and middling classes, and the life of a clerk in one of these shops is perpetual motion. I questioned young men and young women in these shops as to how they liked their work, and as to why they did not try to get into something that offered them more time and better air. In no case out of twenty or thirty persons whom I addressed as particularly likely to sympathize with the suggestion that such a life in such a place was the life of a dog, did I meet with a responsive note. It seemed to these people that all was right; it was a case of where "ignorance is bliss."

I remember again passing through Grand Street early one morning last summer, on my way to take the train for a far-off country village. The morning was intensely uncomfortable, the forerunner of a terrible day, sure to count its victims by the score. In front of every shop along this thoroughfare were groups of clerks busy piling up dry goods in more or less artistic shape, intended to impress the passers. I saw hundreds of men, many of them gray-headed and able-bodied, who seemed to find nothing unpleasant about their work. To one or two I ventured the remark as I went along that it was going to be a very hot day, and that the country boys had the advantage of their city brothers. Even that, the few clerks to whom I spoke were inclined to dispute. The country lad, they argued, had his troubles. It was hot in the cornfield as well as on Grand Street, and while the dry-goods clerk could retire into the depths of the shop, the farm lad had to work away. I found no one inclined to prefer the life of field work to which I looked forward to that of the Grand Street dry-goods shops. These young gentlemen would carry nothing with them should they abandon the shop and their equally empty-headed associates. Why should they give up the society they knew for the utter solitude of a life on the farm, or the bay?

I have put some words of Thoreau's upon the title-page of this book, and no one who has taken the pains to dip into its pages can have failed to see that I have read the famous hermit of Walden Pond with persistency and admiration. There has always been to me something fascinating about this out-door idealist. I never have been, and probably never shall be, a sympathizer with the view which

makes Thoreau a skulker, as Carlyle calls him,
or a loafer, as most of our typical American
business men, if they know any thing about
him at all, would probably dub him.   At the
same time, I will confess that the man's asceticism has less fascination for me than the persistency with which he harps upon the idea
that nine tenths or ninety-nine one-hundredths
of our people waste their time in making money;
touch Thoreau at any point with regard to
business policy or business life, and he fairly
bristles with sarcasm and jibes.   It has been a
life-long wonder to me that the man has not
been valued more highly even in this community devoted to matters of fact, and that so
few outside of a narrow circle of writers and
thinkers know any thing about him.   I am convinced that the time will come when the name
of Henry David Thoreau will stand high in
American annals.   He was our first noted Protestant—passionate, earnest, persistent, honest,
—against the sordid materialism of this country.   Our earlier years as a nation were naturally taken up with hard material work, and if
to-day we place work, as work, upon a pedestal
which it does not deserve, it is due to the heredit-

ary warp of the last one hundred years, when the drawing of water and the hewing of wood were essential to life, to say nothing of comfort. There was certain to be some energetic protest against the narrow view of life which all work and no play was sure to produce in us as a people, and the wonder is that Thoreau stands alone as a protestant.

The personality of the man is so interesting that I will take the liberty of devoting a few pages to saying something of him, using many words and expressions which I find in an admirable little article contributed some years ago to the *Cornhill Magazine*, by Stevenson. "Thoreau's thin, penetrating, big-nosed face, even in a bad wood-cut," says this writer, "conveys some hint of the limitations of his mind and character. With his almost acid sharpness of insight, with his almost animal dexterity in action, there went none of that large, unconscious geniality of the world's hero. He was not easy, or ample, or urbane, not even kind." "He was bred to no profession," says Emerson; "he never married; he lived alone, he went to no church; he never voted, he refused to pay a tax to the State; he ate no flesh, he drank no wine, he never knew the use of tobacco; and though a naturalist, he used neither trap or gun. When asked at dinner what dish he preferred, he answered, 'the nearest.'" He was no ascetic, rather an epicurean of the noblest sort. And he had this one great merit, that he succeeded so far as to be happy. He was content in living like the plant he had planted and watered with solicitude. For instance, he explains his abstinence from tea and coffee by saying that it was bad economy and worthy of no true virtuoso to spoil the natural rapture of the morning with stimulants; let him see the sunshine and he was ready for the labors of the day. These labors were partly to keep out of the way of the world. His faculties were of a piece with his moral shyness. He could guide himself about the woods on the darkest night by the touch of his feet. He could pick up an exact dozen of pencils by feeling; pace distances with accuracy. His smell was so dainty that he could perceive the *fœtor* of dwelling-houses as he passed them at night; his palate so unsophisticated that like a child he disliked the taste of wine; and his knowledge of nature was so complete and curious that he could have told the time of year within a day or so by the aspect of the plants. There were few things that he could not do. He could make a house, a boat, a pencil, or a book. He was a surveyor, a scholar, a natural historian. He could run, walk, climb, skate, and swim, and manage a boat. The smallest occasion served to display his physical accomplishments; and a manufacturer, upon observing his dexterity with the window of a railway car, offered him a situation on the spot.

Thoreau decided from the first to live a life of self-improvement; he saw duty and inclination in that direction. He had no money, and it was a sore necessity which compelled him to make money—even the little he needed. There was a love of freedom, a strain of the wild man in his nature that rebelled with violence against the yoke of custom; he was so eager to cultivate himself and to be happy in his own society, that he could consent with difficulty even to interruptions of friendship. "*Such are my engagements to myself* that I dare not promise," he once wrote in answer to an invitation; and the italics are his own. Thoreau is always

careful of himself, and he must think twice
about a morning call. Imagine him condemned
for eight hours a day to some uncongenial and
unmeaning business.   He shrank from the very
look of the mechanical in life; all should, if
possible, be sweetly spontaneous. Thus he
learned to make lead-pencils, and when he had
gained the highest certificate and his friends
began to congratulate him on his establishment
in life, he calmly announced that he should
never make another. "Why should I," said
he; "I would not do again what I have done
once." Yet in after years, when it became
needful to support his family, he turned
patiently to this mechanical art. He tried
school-teaching. "As I did not teach for the
benefit of my fellow-men," he says, "but simply
for a livelihood, this was a failure." He tried
trade with the same results. As I have already said, his contempt for business and business men was utter. He says: "If our mer-
chants did not most of them fail and the banks
too, my faith in the old rules of this world
would be staggered. The statement that ninety-
nine in a hundred doing such business surely
break down is perhaps the sweetest fact that

statistics have revealed." The wish was probably father to the figures. *Not much! the figu*

"The cost of a thing," says Thoreau, "is
the amount of what I will call life which is
required to be exchanged for it, immediately or
in the long run." The idea may be commonplace, and yet most of us will admit a leavening
of truth in it while declining to make an experiment. Do you want one thousand a year,
or two thousand a year? Do you want ten
thousand a year? And can you afford what
you want? It is a matter of taste, and within
certain lines not in the least a question of duty,
although commonly supposed to be so. There is
no authority for that view anywhere. Thoreau's
tastes are well defined. He loved to be free, to
be master of his times and seasons; he preferred
long rambles to rich dinners, his own reflections
to the consideration of society, and an easy,
calm, unfettered life among green trees to dull
toiling at the counter of a bank. And such
being his inclination, he determined that he
would gratify it.

In 1845, when twenty-eight years old, an age
by which the liveliest of us have usually de-
clined into some conformity with the world,

Thoreau, with a capital of less than twenty-five dollars, and a borrowed axe, walked into the woods by Walden Pond, and began his experiment. He built himself a dwelling, and returned the axe, he says, sharper than when he borrowed it; he reclaimed a patch of ground where he cultivated beans, peas, potatoes, and sweet-corn; he had his bread to bake, his farm to dig, and for six weeks in the summer he worked as surveyor or carpenter. For more than five years this was all that he required to do for his support. For six weeks of occupation, a little cooking and a little gentle hygienic gardening, the man had as good as stolen his living. Or it must rather be allowed that he had done far better; for the thief himself was continually and busily occupied. He says: "What old people tell you you cannot do, you try and find you can." And his conclusion is: "I am convinced that to maintain one's self on this earth is not a hardship but a pastime if we will live simply and wisely; the pursuits of simpler nations are still the sports of the more artificial." When Thoreau had had enough of Walden Pond, he showed the same simplicity in giving it up as in beginning. He made no fetish of his scheme, and did what he wanted squarely. The frugality he exercised and his asceticism are not the notable points of this notable experiment. The remarkable part of it is his recognition of the position of money; he had perceived and was acting on a truth of universal application. A certain amount of money, varying with the number and extent of our desires, is a necessity to each one of us in the present order of society; but beyond that amount, money is a commodity to be bought or not to be bought, a luxury in which we may indulge or stint ourselves like any other. And there are many luxuries that we may legitimately prefer to money, such as a grateful conscience, a country life, or the woman of our inclination. Trite, flat, and obvious as this conclusion may appear, we have only to look around us to see how scantily it has been recognized; and after a little reflection perhaps we may decide to spend a trifle less for money and indulge ourselves a trifle more in freedom.

Says Thoreau: "To have done any thing by which you earned money merely, is to be idle and worse." There are in his letters two passages relating to firewood which illustrate curiously the man's habits and instinct of studying causes and reasons rather than effects. He says: "I suppose I have burned up a good-sized tree to-night—and for what? I settled with Mr. Tarbell for it the other day; but that was n't a final settlement. I got off cheaply from him. At last one will say: 'Let us see, how much wood did you burn, sir?' and I shall shudder to think that the next question will be: 'What did you do while you were warm?'" It is not enough to have earned our livelihood. Either the earning should have been serviceable to mankind or something else must follow. To live is sometimes difficult, but it is never meritorious in itself, and we must have a reason to give our own conscience why we should continue to exist upon this earth. Again he says, speaking of his wood: "There is a far more important and warming heat, commonly lost, which precedes the burning of the wood. It is the smoke of industry, which is incense. I had been so thoroughly warmed in body and spirit that when at length my fuel was housed I came near selling it to the ashman as if I had extracted all its heat." Thus Thoreau was not an idler by any means. Industry was a passion with him, but it must be productive industry. There is not a day when Thoreau does not record some useful work in his diary. He writes, he works his garden, he chops down trees, he helps others. The art he loved was literature. He believed in good books; his reading was not particularly wide, for he hated libraries and had not money wherewith to buy books. In one of his diaries he recalls his indisposition to go to Cambridge or Boston in order to look at books in the library, and he suggests that libraries should be built in the woods where sensitive men might enjoy their contents without being compelled to face the noise and dust of the towns. He wrote at all times; in the evening at his desk, or during a moment's rest upon a fallen log or stone. He composed as he walked, the length of his walk making the length of his writing. When he could not get out-of-doors during the day, for one reason or another, he wrote nothing; he said that houses were like hospitals, and the atmosphere of them enervated the mind as well as the body. His great subjects, the text which he viewed on all sides and was always preaching from, was the pursuit of self-improvement even in the face of unfriendly criticism as it goes on in our society. He was a critic before a naturalist. His books, such as " Walden," and " A Week on the Concord," would be delightful studies of nature even without the touch of interest they acquire at the thought that the man himself is preaching to an audience of people who consider him little better than a madman. Unquestionably he was a true lover of nature.

The quality which we should call mystery in a painting, and which belongs so particularly to the aspect of the external world and to its influence upon our feelings, was one which he was never weary of attempting to reproduce in his books. The significance of nature's appearances, their unchanging strangeness to the senses and the thrilling response they awaken in the mind of man continued to surprise and stimulate his spirits. He writes to a friend: "Let me suggest a theme for you—to state to yourself precisely and completely what that walk over the mountains amounted to for you, returning to this essay again and again until you are satisfied that all that was important in your experience is in it. Don't suppose that you record it precisely the first dozen times you try, but at 'em again ; especially when, after a sufficient pause you suspect that you are touching the heart·or stomach of the matter. Reiterate your blows there and account for the mountain to yourself. Not that the story need be long, but it will take a long while to make it short." Perhaps the most successful work that Thoreau accomplished in this direction is to be found in the passages relating to fish in the "Week." These are remarkable for a vivid truth of impression and a happy use of language not frequently surpassed.

Perhaps the very coldness and egoism of his own nature gave Thoreau a clearer insight into the intellectual basis of our warm mutual tolerations grouped under the head of friendship ; testimony to the value of friendship comes with added force from one who was solitary and disobliging, and of whom a friend remarked : " I love Henry, but I cannot like him." He made scarcely any distinction between love and friendship. He was, indeed, too accurate an observer not to remark that there exists already a natural disinterestedness and liberality between men and women ; yet he thought friendship no re-

specter of sex. "We are not what we are,"
says he, "nor do we treat or esteem each other
for such but for what we are capable of being."
Again : "It is the merit and preservation of
friendship that it takes place on a higher level
than the actual characters of the parties would
seem to warrant. Is this not light in a dark
place? We are different with different friends;
yet if we look closer, we shall find that every
such relation reposes on some particular hy-
pothesis of one's self." Yet this analyst of
friendship was not friendly with many persons and was intimate with none. Thoreau
had no illusions; he does not give way to love
any more than to hatred, but preserves them
both with care, like valuable curiosities. He is
an egoist; he does not remember that in these
near intimacies we are ninety-nine times disappointed in our beggarly selves for once that we
are disappointed in our friends; that it is we
who seem most frequently undeserving of the
love that unites us. Thoreau is after profit in
these intimacies; moral profit, to be sure, but
still profit to himself. "If you will be the sort
of friend I want," he remarks, "my education
cannot dispense with your society." As though

his friend were a dictionary. And with all this,
not one word about pleasure, or laughter, or
kisses, or any quality of flesh and blood. It
was not inappropriate, surely, that he had such
close relations with the fishes. We can understand the friend already quoted when he cried:
" As for taking his arm, I would as soon think
of taking the arm of an elm tree." It is not
surprising that he experienced but a broken
enjoyment in his intimacies; he went to see
his friends as one might stroll in to see a cricket-
match—not simply for the pleasure of the
thing, but with some afterthought of self-
improvement. It was his theory that people
saw each other too frequently; they had nothing fresh to communicate; friendship with him
meant a society for mutual improvement.

" The only obligation," says he, " which I
have a right to assume is to do at any time
what I think right." " Why should we ever go
abroad, even across the way to ask a neighbor's
advice?" " There is a nearer neighbor within
who is incessantly telling us how we should be-
have. But we wait for the neighbor without to
tell us of some faults." " The greater part of
what my neighbors call good I believe in my

soul to be bad." To be what we are and to become what we are capable of becoming is the end
of life. It is "when we fall behind ourselves,"
that "we are cursed with duties and the neglect
of duties." "I love the wild," he says, "not less
than the good." The life of a good man will
hardly improve us more than the life of a free-
booter, for the inevitable laws appear as plainly
in the infringement as in the observance, and
our lives are sustained by a nearly equal expense
of virtue of some kind." "As for doing good,"
he writes elsewhere, "that is one of the professions that are full. Moreover, I have tried it
fairly, and, strange as it may seem, am satisfied
that it does not agree with my constitution.
Probably I should not conscientiously and delib-
erately forsake my particular calling to do the
good which society demands of me to save the
universe from annihilation ; and I believe that
a like but infinitely greater steadfastness elsewhere is all that preserves it now. If you should
ever be betrayed into any of these philanthro-
pies, do not let your left hand know what your
right hand does, for it is not worth knowing."

In the case of Thoreau so great a show of
doctrine contrary to what the world believed,

demanded some practical outcome. If nothing were to be done but build a shanty at Walden Pond, we have heard too much of these declarations of independence. That the man wrote some books is nothing to the purpose, for the same has been done in a suburban villa. That he kept himself happy is perhaps a sufficient excuse, but it is disappointing to the reader. We may be unjust, but when a man despises commerce and philanthropy and has views of good so soaring that he must take himself apart from mankind for their cultivation, we will not rest content without some striking act. And it was not Thoreau's fault if he were not martyred; had the occasion come, he would have made a noble ending. He made one practical appearance on the stage of affairs, and strangely characteristic of the man. It was forced on him by his calm but radical opposition to negro slavery. " Voting for the right is doing nothing for it," he says; " it is only expressing to men feebly your desire that it should prevail." " I do not hesitate to say," he adds, " that those who call themselves abolitionists should at once effectually withdraw their support both in person and property from the government of Massachusetts." This is what he did. In 1843 he ceased to pay the poll tax. He had seceded. He says: " In fact I declare war with the State after my own fashion." He was put in prison, but that was a part of his design. "Under a government which imprisons any un- justly, the true place for a just man is also in prison. I know this well, that if one thousand, if one hundred, if ten men whom I could name —ay, if one honest man in this State of Massa- chusetts, ceasing to hold slaves, were actually to withdraw from this copartnership and be locked up in the county jail therefor it would be the abolition of slavery in America." A friend paid the tax for him and continued year by year to pay it, so that Thoreau was free to walk the woods.

This curious personality of Henry David Thoreau stands alone, apparently, as a practical attempt to grasp the good things of this world, in a higher sense, without paying the penalty which tradition and custom exact. In more ways than in money we constantly pay for the privilege of living in crowds. To say nothing of the nervous wear and tear, the whole drift is by association tending towards deterioration.

So long as we continue to live in crowds
there must be an infinite amount of contact
with human nature which is petty, mean,
despicable. We cannot escape from it. While
in Rome we must do as the Romans. I confess
that if my fellow-man is typified in the crowd
I see around me, especially in large cities, I
detest my fellow-man. It may be the height
of selfishness for the egoist to say: "These
people have nothing good to teach me; I can
gain nothing from them; let them keep to
themselves and allow me to strive for something higher, untrammelled by their association,
or their advice." But such a course may be wise
in order to make the most of what little capital we have fallen heir to in the shape of health,
intelligence, and appreciation of things which are
priceless in every sense, such as the sunlight
and the color of the clouds. To get rid of unpleasant and seemingly unprofitable associa-
tions Thoreau cut loose from society and buried
himself at Walden. You may call it selfishness, if you will, but which is more likely to
occur: that you will sink to the level of the
crowd which surrounds you, or that, by taking
up your cross and remaining at your post, the

crowd will benefit by your self-sacrifices and reflect one gleam of what you may consider to be your superior light? Is there not egoism in either course, perhaps the lesser in fleeing from the crowd and trying to work out salvation for one's self and one's family?

See John Borroughs' essay
on Thoreau in his "Indoor
Studies". —

The most sympathetic as well
as most rational study of
Thoreau which I know of is the
"Life of Henry David Thoreau by H.
S. Salt, London, Bentley, 1896

WHAT WE LOSE AND WHAT WE GAIN.

WHEN the prisoners were released from the Bastille by the mob, it is said that some of the old men begged to be allowed to return to their cells; they had become so accustomed to darkness and confinement that they dreaded the open air. The man who can find nothing but ennui in the fields is an illustration of the same curious phenomenon—the loss of appreciation of what is best in life. For several years I have been harping upon this theme; I have preached in season and out of season, that open-air life is the right one, and that any man who ties himself down for eight or ten hours a day the year round to a desk, is paying too much for the money he earns; and I have done this without, so far as I know, making a single convert. I have preached country life and country work until some of my friends dread the mention of the subject. In the beginning they argued the matter; now they laugh, as if

to say that I have become so infatuated with
my hobby as to have lost all sense of proportion.   I never expected to make a convert; in
fact, I should feel rather uncomfortable if any
friend of mine should desert his desk and take
to the garden for a living upon my advice.
So that I have not been disappointed.   At the
same time, I have discovered nothing to make
me doubt the soundness of my position.   I
listen to ridicule and argument, endeavoring to
give due weight to what I hear.   The chief
reasons why this desertion of the town is de-
nounced as folly may be summed up as follows:
(1) The loneliness of the country will become
oppressive; (2) it will be impossible to give my
family more than the comforts of a workman's
home—our living will be plain, our clothes will
be unfashionable, our rich neighbors will not
call upon us; (3) the children will grow up no
better than farmers' children; (4) in the end
there will be a return to town to take up the
old life under conditions of greater hardship
than ever, years of absence having broken con-
nections that might have become profitable
with time; (5) to leave town for good, or practically for good, is unfair to my wife and chil-

dren, even if I do find pleasure and profit
myself in such a step. It is implied that life
without new bonnets is not worth living to a
woman, and that children may grow up to be
young savages. In the following pages I try
to answer these objections. Whether or not I
succeed in convincing any one, I am sure that
they rest upon a wholly false estimate of the
value of city life and upon the equally false
notion to the effect that intellectual growth
cannot take place far from great cities. One of
my acquaintances to whom I announced one
day that I hoped never again to spend more
than ten weeks of the year in the city, said to
me: " How do you get on without society?
In summer you may have city friends glad to
share your bluefish and honey for a few weeks,
but the rest of the year—before July and after
September—it must be lonely enough to drive
you crazy."

So I must hear the talk of the town in order
to be happy? Seriously, I do not believe that
from one end of the week to the other passed
in the very heart of the city's turmoil, working
for many hours in a busy newspaper office—
the very place where interesting talk is sup-

posed to centre—visiting a club or two, going
to the theatre and to the opera several times—
I do not believe that in this busy week I hear
enough interesting talk to compensate me for
the loss of one hour in my orchard or on the
bay. You cannot get out of people what is
not in them. You cannot expect the successful dealer in butter, sugar, or candle-grease
to tell you any thing you do not know, unless
it is about things he buys and sells, and I am
not interested in these things. Of all the dreary
stuff with which our dreary newspapers are
filled, by all odds the most dreary to me consists of the reproductions of the talk of these
good people. The personal-gossip column,
which of late years has grown to great lengths
—millionaire A's explanation of the recent rise
in the price of leather, Senator B's reason's for
believing that Coroner Jones will again be
elected this year, are matters that do not interest me in the least. An ocean of gabble
which to-day appears to hide the paucity of
ideas among us has broken into the newspapers.
The exaggeration of trifles is one of the dis-
eases of the age. The instructions given to
our reporters seem to be to question the boot-

black who blacks their shoes, the washerwoman
who brings home their shirts, and the President
of the United States, if they are lucky enough
to meet him, printing all that the washerwoman,
the boot-black, and the President, may have to
say about their respective businesses. The
stuff is ground over and over again. Nothing
interesting can come from people who have no
ideas, and ideas do not come by dint of gabble.
Silence is golden. In my orchard there is
silence. I have always admired Webster's reply
to a barber, who asked him how he wished to
be shaved. " In silence," replied the great man.
I suppose that I am told a dozen times a day
by different persons that it is a fine day, or a
wet day, or that it was cold yesterday, or will
rain to-morrow. The boy who opens the door
for me as I leave my house gives me his opinion as to the weather, the man who runs the
elevator downtown does the same thing, the
waiter who brings me some luncheon gives me
his views on the weather, past, present, and
future, and as I ride home the conductor, if he
finds time, tells me what kind of weather we are
having. At the risk of seeming crusty to a
degree I will confess that I care for no man's

opinion about the weather, unless it is the government expert's, and not much for his.

It is assumed that in town one meets with people who have ideas—authors, writers, thinkers, men of science, whose words are full of inspiration. Perhaps I have been rather fortunate in meeting with people whose names are heard frequently. Yet I cannot say that the loss of such opportunities as I have enjoyed in this respect ever worries me. Take the authors and the writers, for instance. The man who has time and leisure may occasionally, if he likes that sort of thing, meet the author whose novels are most read at the moment. But it is extremely doubtful whether this gentleman will talk half so well in the drawing-room as he does in his book. These authors are devoting the best part of their lives to thinking of something brilliant wherewith to amuse me; they polish their work, going over it scores of times, finally presenting it to me nicely printed and illustrated, if necessary. And I may listen as long or as little as I like to what they may have to say. In days when there were no such thing as cheap printing and magazines, I suppose that the talk of the town was essential to many people. To-day, the author who has a clever idea sells it. The very dependence upon gossip for ideas betrays lack of reading. When for a few cents we can buy the results of the best thinking of our best writers, why should we run after the writers themselves? Of course I am not talking about what men of high position in the literary world or the social world may be able to get out of the life of cities; I am speaking of what the poor man, hard driven to earn the few thousand dollars a year needed to keep his children in bread and butter, will probably, judging by my own experience and that of some of my friends, be able to think of as a possible loss in considering the advisability of deserting the city for the country.

I am not sure but that we enjoy the work of some men all the better because we do not know them personally. At a distance they are heroes, more or less. I have heard some people say that their enjoyment in the magic of Richard Wagner's works would be unquestionably deepened had they not had the misfortune to meet the man himself—a great genius who was utterly indifferent to what people thought of him, and utterly careless of the

wounds he inflicted.   I esteem it rather a piece
of good fortune that I never saw the greatest
musician that the world has ever seen or probably will see for generations to come.   The
personality of the man was not a pleasant one,
and I believe that I am justified in saying this,
notwithstanding some attempts to make out a
different case.   A famous Leipsic lawyer, a
Jew, has in his study a marble bust of Wagner,
with a wreath of laurel on its brow and a rope
around its neck.   " The one," he says to visitors, " shows what I think of the composer, the
other what I think of the man."   And the Jews
are not alone in their detestation of the man,
while confessing to an unlimited admiration for
the musician.   His pamphlets against the Jew
in music, his caricatures of the French in de-
feat, were only a small part of the offensive,
wounding things that Wagner allowed himself
to utter.   The anecdotes of the man's arro-
gance are many.   I know of one young American who would enjoy Wagner's music more
had he never attempted to interview the composer of " Tristan."   This particular enthusiast
had been sent by one of our newspapers to
Bayreuth for the express purpose of telling

Wagner how much the great world of America delighted in the master's works, and to get from him some sort of pleasant acknowledgment, if possible, of the courtesy. The scribe arrived in Bayreuth and wasted a score of cards and letters without obtaining the promise of an interview. The situation was becoming desperate —his newspaper wanted an interview. The young man learned that Wagner was accustomed to stroll every morning in a certain wood soon after sunrise. He waylaid the composer and found him seated upon a bench. Now Wagner did not love newspapers or newspaper men, and he had good reason. But surely an exception might be made in favor of America. There he had not been attacked or ridiculed by newspaper men, for the very good reason that his name was scarcely known, to say nothing of his music. The interviewer made a bold attack. Mustering up his best German, he began his address, Wagner gazing dreamily at him and not moving a muscle: "I am commissioned by a great newspaper of that great Republic over the seas, where your music is already a household word (!), to tell you of the deep admiration that exists for you there, and to ask

you for some words of greeting in return." Not
a word did the great man vouch in reply. Perhaps he failed to catch my meaning, thought
the young man ; and so he repeated his little
speech.   Then Wagner pointed towards the
gates of the park, muttering a few German
words, a free but fair translation of which might
be—" Get out ! "   While this was not the sort
of interview which had been hoped for, it did not
prevent the interviewer from making a column
talk with Wagner, in which the composer was
made to bubble over with gratitude to America
and Americans.   Those in the secret knew that
the interview upon Wagner's part consisted of
but two words.   I am not defending the institution of interviewing, and I do not doubt that
Wagner may have had excellent reasons for ob-
jecting to such an intrusion ; the world may
have lost some musical thought of the utmost
beauty by the enterprise, so-called, of this
American ; I am simply giving an illustration
of what may be lost by too near a view of a
great man.

The art of writing most beautifully upon
charity may exist in a man whose life knows
not a charitable instinct or act.   The man who

can talk and write exquisitely about love towards one's neighbor may be conspicuous for a vile temper at home. The novelist who delights me in print may, and probably will, disappoint me in person. Upon the whole, while I can look back to some pleasure derived from the talk of men whose writings are famous, I doubt whether the disappointments do not outweigh the pleasures. Certainly the satisfaction which I have found in meeting persons who write well has been infinitesimal as compared with the pleasure which these same persons have given me by their books. As to the so-called literary evenings of great cities—occasions upon which some person in public view at the moment is placed upon exhibition by Mrs. Leo Hunter, I know of few less dreary ways of wasting precious time.

I presume that in this matter of house, grounds, clothes, and other signs of outward luxury, the fact that poverty is considered synonymous with inferiority is primarily due to simple causes. I wear a patched coat; therefore I have no money wherewith to buy a new one. The absence of money implies inability to earn money; therefore I am not so energetic

or so clever as some of my fellow-men who earn
more money and wear good coats.   In a country where the measure of a man is the amount
of money or property that he has been able to
acquire, either through industry or luck in gambling, it is inevitable that the money standard, or the coat standard, should acquire the
weight of a moral law.   The man who wears a
patched coat and only wears gloves when the
weather makes the gloves a physical comfort,
must be an inferior sort of man, because he has
evidently not kept pace with his fellows in the
race.   In the Old World the struggle for money
and material prosperity has not been so exhausting these last few hundred years, and has not
excluded spiritual things so completely as with
us ; and there we find, in consequence, that the
outward signs of the ability to earn money are
not deemed so essential to the fixing of a man's
standing in the community.   To wear a patched
coat and to work with one's hands in a garden,
do not in themselves stamp a man in France
and England as an inferior person.   I was particularly impressed with this when some years
ago an English clergyman—a man of much culture and reading—gave up his cure in a fashion-

able summer resort not a thousand miles from
New York, because he found that his love of
working his own garden was looked upon with
surprise, to use no stronger term, and he was
made to feel that his parishioners considered the
dignity of their church endangered by their
pastor's curious fancy for digging. In England
it had been his custom to raise his own vegetables. Here it was not thought dignified for the
pastor to work like a common laborer, hanging his coat on a bramble bush, and one of his
vestry-men hinted that the church might be
able to squeeze out enough money to provide a
gardener for the pastor. The pastor did not
want a gardener, and he gave way to some one
else who would keep his coat on and his hands
clean. It may be said that instead of resign-
ing his place, this victim of the Philistines
should have preached a few sermons upon the
dignity of manual labor, recalling the fact that
Christ was a carpenter; but the depth of such
prejudice is beyond the plummet of argument.
The commonplace mind is never tolerant of
other views. For years manual labor, because it
does not bring in much money, has been looked
upon as the work of the inferior man ; the am-

bition of every one has been to get away from it.   The farmer's son deserts the farm ; the carpenter's son leaves the bench ; any occupation which allows a man to wear a coat and keep his hands white is considered better than manual labor.   It is commonly considered that of all the occupations farming pays the least money in proportion to the care and labor expended. Therefore farming and gardening must be the last occupation that a man of parts will take up.   To devote hours to digging or gardening or any work which a laborer at a dollar a day will accomplish as well, is considered folly when a dollar an hour can be earned at other work.   If the accumulation of money is the end of life, I suppose that public opinion is right ; but even upon this point it may be doubted whether or not in the long run the man who acquires sound health by systematic out-door work does not stand a better chance in the race for money than nine tenths of his fellow-men.

Dress is not an art founded upon fixed principles of beauty.   What one generation admires the next will ridicule.   Perhaps the time will come when patches will be in fashion.   We already find it possible to admire Oriental rugs in tatters, and vast sums are paid for bits of Persian carpets about to fall in pieces. Does not every one know that should the Prince of Wales appear in public with a shabby coat and a patch upon both knees, that patches would appear upon every fashionable knee, and that unpatched trousers would be viewed with suspicion? There are no end of stories which illustrate how strongly the traits of our simian ancestors are marked in us. Some years ago the Prince of Wales could not find the overcoat he wanted when about to leave for the opera one evening, and picked up a rough shooting-jacket he had brought from the Highlands; result: ulsters appeared all over the world. More recently, the same leader of fashion dropped one glove in the street and put on another of a different color; result: people begin to wear gloves that do not match. The Prince of Wales is growing bald; result: the sale of magic hair-growers has fallen off by two thirds in the United Kingdom. The traces of the monkey are to be seen all around us. Not one man in a thousand knows that the two buttons to be found upon the backs of most coats date from the time when men needed these buttons to hold on their sword-belts. The swords have gone, but we continue to insist upon the buttons because "everybody weàrs them." The necktie once held the shirt together at the throat, and thus served a useful purpose. Buttons now fill the office, but the tie survives, and the man who goes without a necktie is held up to scorn. A score of such customs which have now no other warrant than that "every one else does so" might be given. Yet it is more difficult to teach a boy the necessity of truth than the folly of too much attention to his clothes. As things go there is a reason in the present insistance upon fine feathers; the man who wishes to be well paid must make people believe that he is worth large pay and that other people think so. If he is richly dressed, it is a sign that his services have been considered worthy of a rich reward. "It pays to dress well," has become a maxim with us, and there is reason behind it. It does pay—in money. But we must take care that we do not pay too much for that money.

The matter of clothes has been suggested as offering possible obstacles to a life without money, and the topic has been treated so fully,

and so much better by Thoreau than I can
hope to treat it, that I will venture to quote at
length from his " Walden." It is begging the
question to assume that because one may
attempt to get a great deal of life out of comparatively few dollars, the result will be rags
for the family. Thoreau is eloquent upon the
subject of patches, and could see nothing to be
ashamed of in them. Since his day the matter
has been largely simplified for the weaklings
who do not like to excite comment even of
people who have never pondered upon the
beauty of patches. Clothing, and every other
commodity which is largely made by machinery
has been cheapened in proportion to the part
of the work performed by machinery, and every
year this part grows larger and larger. Consequently, the amount of clothing which can be
bought for a day's labor is six or seven times
as great as it was one hundred years ago, and
three or four times as great as when the hermit
of " Walden " jotted down sarcastic notes about
the man who was not ashamed of going around
with a broken leg, but very much ashamed of
a broken pair of trousers. This process is going on so steadily that it is easy to foresee the

day when a few days' work upon the part of
the laborer or mechanic will be sufficient to
provide himself and his family with unpatched
and well-made clothing for the year. I have a
prejudice against patches to the extent of dislik-
ing any thing that will attract the attention of
Tom, Dick, and Harry, and their female counterparts. If for a few dollars spent in clothing
which is whole I can save myself from their
attentions, it is money well spent, and the same
thing holds good with regard to the clothing
of my wife and children. We might spend a
few dollars less every year upon bonnets and
dresses, but the question is : Would it pay? We
are not living in the woods, and our desire
is to avoid attracting attention.

To go back to Thoreau, he says in "Walden":

"As for clothing, to come at once to the
practical part of the question, perhaps we are
led oftener by the love of novelty, and a regard
for the opinions of men in procuring it than by
a true utility. Let him who has work to do
recollect that the object of clothing is, first, to
retain the vital heat, and, secondly, in this state
of society, to cover nakedness, and he may
judge how much of any necessary or important
work may be accomplished without adding to

his wardrobe. Kings and queens who wear a suit but once, though made by some tailor or dressmaker to their majesties, cannot know the comfort of wearing a suit that fits. They are no better than wooden horses to hang the clean clothes on. Every day our garments become more assimilated to ourselves, receiving the impress of the wearer's character, until we hesitate to lay them aside, without such delay and medical appliances and some such solemnity even as our bodies. No man ever stood the lower in my estimation for having a patch in his clothes, yet I am sure that there is greater anxiety, commonly, to have fashionable, or at least clean and unpatched clothes, than to have a sound conscience. But even if the rent is not mended, perhaps the worst vice betrayed is improvidence. I sometimes try my acquaintances by such tests as this: Who would wear a patch, or two extra seams only, over the knee? Most behaved as if they believed that their prospects for life would be ruined if they should do it. It would be easier for them to hobble to town with a broken leg than with a broken pantaloon. Often if an accident happens to a gentleman's legs, they can be mended, but if a similar accident happens to the legs of his pantaloons there is no help for it, for he considers not what is truly respectable but what is respected. We know but few men, a great many coats and breeches. Dress a scarecrow in your last shift, you stand-

ing shiftless by, who would not soonest salute
the scarecrow? Passing a cornfield the other
day close by a hat and coat on a stake, I recognized the owner of the farm. He was only a
little more weather-beaten than when I saw him
last. I have heard of a dog that barked at
every stranger who approached his master's
premises with clothes on, but was easily quieted
by a naked thief. It is an interesting question
how far men would retain their relative rank if
they were divested of their clothes. Could you
in such a case tell surely of any company of
civilized men which belonged to the most respected class? When Madame Pfeiffer, in her
adventurous travels round the world from east
to west, had got so near home as Asiatic Russia
she says she felt the necessity of wearing other
than a travelling dress when she went to meet
the authorities, for she 'was now in a civilized
country where people are judged of by their
clothes!' Even in our democratic New England towns the accidental possession of wealth
and its manifestation in dress and equipage
alone obtain for the possessor almost universal
respect. But they who yield such respect,
numerous as they are, are so far heathen, and
need to have a missionary sent to them.

"A man who has at length found something
to do will not need to get a new suit to do it
in; for him the old will do, that has lain dusty
in the garret for an indeterminate period. Old

shoes will serve a hero longer than they have served his valet—if a hero ever has a valet;— bare feet are older than shoes, and he can make them do. Only they who go to *soirées* and legislative halls must have new coats, coats to change as often as the man changes in them. But if my jacket and trousers, my hat and shoes, are fit to worship God in, they will do, will they not? Who ever saw his old clothes, his old coat actually worn out, resolved into its primitive elements, so that it was not a deed of charity to bestow it on some poor boy, by him, perchance, to be bestowed on one poorer still, or shall we say richer, who could do with less? I say beware of all enterprises that require new clothes and not rather a new wearer of clothes. If there is not a new man, how can the new clothes be made to fit? If you have any enterprise before you, try it in your old clothes. All men want not something to do with, but something to do, or rather something to be. Perhaps we should never procure a new suit, however dirty or ragged the old, until we have so conducted, so enterprised or sailed in some way, that we feel like new men in the old, and that to retain it would be like keeping new wine in old bottles. Our moulting season, like that of the fowls, must be a crisis in our lives. The loon retires to solitary ponds to spend it. Thus, also, the snake casts its slough, and the caterpillar its wormy coat, by an internal indus-

try and expansion; for clothes are but our out-
most cuticle and mortal coil. Otherwise we
shall be found sailing under false colors, and be
inevitably cashiered at last by our own opinion
as well as that of mankind.

"When I ask for a garment of a particular
form, my tailoress tells me gravely: 'They do
not make them so now,' not emphasizing the
'They' at all, as if she quoted an authority as
impersonal as the Fates, and I find it difficult
to get made what I want, simply because she
cannot believe that I mean what I say—that I
am so rash. When I hear this oracular sen-
tence, I am for a moment absorbed in thought,
emphasizing to myself each word separately
that I may come at the meaning of it, that
I may find out by what degree of consanguinity
'They' are related to me, and what authority
they may have in an affair which affects me so
nearly; and, finally, I am inclined to answer
her with equal mystery, and without any more
emphasis on the 'They.' It is true they did
not make them so recently, but they do so
now. We worship not the Graces, nor the
Parcæ, but Fashion. She spins and weaves
and cuts with full authority. The head monkey at Paris puts on a traveller's cap, and all
the monkeys in America do the same. I sometimes despair of getting any thing quite simple
and honest done in this world by the help of
men. They would have to be passed through

a powerful press first, to squeeze their old no-
tions out of them, so that they would not soon
get upon their legs again, and then there would
be some one in the company with a maggot in
his head, hatched from an egg deposited there
nobody knows when, for not even fire kills
these things, and you would have lost your
labor.

"On the whole, I think that it cannot be
maintained that dressing has in this or any
other country risen to the dignity of an art.
At present men make shift to wear what they
can get. Like shipwrecked sailors they put on
what they can find on the beach, and at a little
distance, whether of space or time, laugh at
each other's masquerade. Every generation
laughs at the old fashions, but follows reli-
giously the new. We are amused at beholding
the costume of Henry VIII., or Queen Eliza-
beth, as much as if it was that of the King and
Queen of the Cannibal Islands. All costume
off a man is pitiful or grotesque. It is only the
serious eye peering from and the sincere life
passed within it which restrain laughter and
consecrate the costume of any people. Let
Harlequin be taken with a fit of the colic, and
the trappings will have to serve that mood too.
When the soldier is hit by a cannon-ball, rags
are as becoming as purple. The childish and
savage taste of men and women for new pat-
terns keeps how many shaking and squinting

through kaleidoscopes that they may discover
the particular figure which this generation requires to-day."

In writing of clothing, I wish, however, to
make plain that inexpensive clothes do not
imply shabbiness or carelessness in personal
appearance, but simply that the blouse of the
French workman is better than the dirty linen
shirt of the American workman. To be appro-
priately dressed does not, in these days of cor-
duroys and flannel shirts, cost either much
money or time, and the man who allows himself and his children to go dressed as scarecrows
misses one element for good in country life.
Clothing which may be out of place in town
may become just the thing in the country life,
even though its cost is insignificant as compared to the dress of the city man. Were my
income twenty times as large as it is, I should
not care to dress better than I do. For the
children blue-flannel dresses are cheap, but
could any thing be more appropriate for the
life on the water which they lead?

In one of his books on fishing, Frank Forester
(H. W. Herbert) says that if he led the life of
a backwoodsman, and dwelt in a cabin on top

of a mountain, he should still put on evening dress for dinner. This is an exaggeration, but there is truth behind. Slovenly, ill-fitting, dirty, ragged clothing may lead to slovenly habits of mind, and are not the necessary accompaniments of such life as I prescribe.

One of my critics, for whom I have great personal deference, tells me that my theory of life tends to a relapse into barbarism, and in illustration of the truth of his position, he pointed one evening to a music-stand near the piano with the remark: " With your ideas, that stand would never be made of mahogany and elaborately ornamented, but would be of pine, perhaps stained."

Well, suppose it was. I am inclined to think that the greater use of common material, stained pine and other cheap wood, in the houses of people of taste is a distinct indication of a needed reform. Take the little music-stand in illustration. Its purpose is to hold a number of music-books and loose sheets of music. It has three or four shelves, and is so made as to stand in a corner near the piano and take up but little room. It is made of mahogany, highly polished, and is ornamented, as most people would call it, with a sort of stucco-beading, which to me is distasteful. But it cost money, and therefore has its reasons for being in certain eyes. I have forgotten what it cost me—probably from fifteen to twenty dollars. Thanks to the growth of good taste, I can to-day pick out from half-a-dozen books I know of a little design for a music-stand, or sketch it myself, and the nearest carpenter will make the thing in a day at a cost of two or three dollars for wood, labor, and staining. The result will be something which is pleasanter to my eye, and I will venture to say to the eyes of nine out of ten persons of educated taste. The other fifteen or sixteen dollars saved may be devoted to books, pictures, music—any of the things which really add something to life. The music-stand of stained pine will do its work just as well as the one made of mahogany, inlaid with stucco beading—in fact it will do it better, for it will not need a periodic rubbing on the part of the parlor-maid to keep it bright and polished, and it can be moved about when occasion demands, as it weighs but little. It is as strong as the other, and it will last a hundred years.

The music-stand is typical of the whole theory upon which I have preached so persistently and to some extent practised. In every affair of life, we have been insisting upon mahogany, with stucco trimmings, and wasting money which might have gone far towards buying books and sunlight. It is a hopeful sign when we find the saving remnant, as Matthew Arnold has it, taking to stained pine instead of mahogany with stucco trimmings. I have a sincere love for pretty things. I will walk a mile to see a set of china exquisitely decorated. Some Persian rugs give me as much pleasure as many pictures. A noble house is something that I should like to own. But there has always been the question: Is it going to pay me to have china at my table which costs one hundred dollars, or a rug before the fire which costs half as much again? It is all a question of whether I will give up something else. Shall I exchange a week of sunlight for the sake of that dinner service, and another week for the sake of that rug, and another month for the sake of living in the house which pleases me, and so on. After weighing the losses and the gains pretty carefully, I say No.

A far more serious objection which is made to my plan of life is that it is not fair to my children. I have had the advantage of good schools, I have been sent abroad to study, I have had years of life among people who know something of books and art. It may be very well for me to desert from the ranks, and settle down in the woods, intellectually speaking, of this end of Long Island. This is a serious question. Had I never conceived the idea of seceding, I should at this time be paying rent for a little house or an apartment in some part of New York City, or what is more likely I should live most of the year in some of the little settlements, within easy railroad distance from New York, which dot the Jersey hills. Years ago, before my eyes were opened, I paid seven hundred dollars a year for a cottage in just such a settlement. With that expense and the cost of three months' board in New York, for newspaper work makes it necessary for me to be in New York at least that length of time, I may say that my rent was about a thousand dollars, a moderate sum, and yet large enough, when taken in connection with the other expenses of servants and housekeeping, to necessitate pretty steady drudgery upon my part the year round. In the meantime, my children attended a little school which was quite as good as any preparatory school of the same type to be found in the city.

From the experience that I have had with children's schools, I have been led to think that the most pretentious are often the least productive of any good to the child, and I presume that most parents will agree in condemning the ultra-fashionable and most expensive schools as wonderfully well designed to make a child all that it should not be. With the primary schools there is scarcely any choice to be made between those of the city and the country. The home life of the child before twelve years of age counts for so much in forming the character and the intellectual judgment of the child that schools, good or bad, are not of great weight. If any thing, the little, unpretentious district school of the smallest country village is better than the city school, because there are fewer children, and consequently their idiosyncrasies are more likely to have full play. The worst that can be said of our public-school system is that it tends to eliminate

individuality and make each child the counter-
part of the standard child, often a very low
standard.   At the most impressionable age,
we send our children to schools in which the
effort is to turn out boys and girls all knowing
the same thing, taking the same view of every
topic, and approaching more closely to a type
with which educated persons have really very
little sympathy.   It is a standard in which the
commonplace dominates.   Matthew Arnold attributed the uninteresting character and monotony of much of the casual talk which he
heard in our public places to the universal custom of sending children to the public schools.
Spencer holds that there is no harm, but rather
good, in allowing a child to grow up a healthy
animal almost ignorant of ordinary school rudi-
ments until he reaches the age of eight or ten.
By that time it is to be hoped that he will be
less plastic, and that the influence of home
surroundings will have brought out an individuality not to be effaced by the routine schooling
of the next few years.   The tendency to do
away with book lessons for young children has
always seemed to me one of the healthiest
signs of the day, and with my own children

I have had no compunctions of conscience in teaching them to swim and row and to love fishing and hunting before they knew how to read or write a line. The worst that could happen to them would be to have them turn out to be counterparts of the commonplace type I find in most of the public schools. The boy who at the age of twelve is a good swimmer, a good sailor, fond of shooting, fishing, and out-door sports, is able to read and write, and has a genuine love and appreciation of a score of good books, and not a little good music, is pretty sure to get along in whatever school he finds himself, for whatever he knows, he will know thoroughly and not superficially.

The real school is, after all, the home school, of which the father and mother are the head teachers. Here, again, is one reason why life in the wilderness is an advantage to the child. He is with his father most of the day, and if the household has any atmosphere of culture about it, he is pretty sure to absorb some of it. In city life, the father may be seen at break-fast, and possibly for a moment before the children go to bed, but that, as a rule, is all, except on Sunday, when he is often too tired to

bother with the children and too unfamiliar
with them to take much interest in their doings.   More than half the pleasure that I get
out of my country life is due to constant association with the children.   The boat seldom
sails away without three or four of them on
board, they are never left behind when we
start for a day's outing, they know as much
about the garden as I do, and probably to this
active open-air life they owe largely their
strength and ruddy cheeks.   I have tried both
ways of life, and whatever may be said in favor
of the city so far as adults are concerned, there
are no two ways of thinking so far as concerns
the children.   After a few years, when it becomes necessary to fit them for active life, I
suppose that the boys will go to college, and I
am not at all afraid of their ability to hold
their own and to get all the good that may be
obtained by a struggle for wealth if they should
choose to strive for it.   As to the girls, it may
be said that in the wilderness they would grow
up ignorant of most accomplishments valued
in young women, such as music, painting, etc.
But here again, it is a question of home influence.   Inasmuch as my girls will hear at home

twenty times as much good music as the average New York girl even in fashionable life
is likely to hear, and a hundred times as much
talk about it, there is no fear that if they have
any capacity for the divine art, it will not make
itself felt.   It is so rare to find among even our
so-called best people of the town any under-
standing or appreciation of the meaning and
beauty of literature, music, and art, that the
fear that my children may not know something
of these things because they do not habitually
associate with these so-called best people,
seems really comical to me.   The well-to-do
people of the city will spend money upon any
thing but art ; they will cheerfully lavish dollars upon mahogany furniture with stucco
veneering, but it will never occur to them to
try pine and have their children taught to
understand a Beethoven sonata.   It has been
said that under such a system as mine my
boys are likely to grow up fishermen, and
nothing more, and that my girls will probably
know how to make good butter.   Even taking
this material view of the matter, I am not at
all sure but that an intelligent fisherman who
lives in comfort the year round, harassed by

no anxieties, and getting the most out of the sea-breeze and the sunlight, has not a far better lot than his city brother who wears more expensive clothes and talks about the price of lard or leather instead of the fish and the tides. As to the essentials of intellectual culture, the fisherman with a taste for reading and his long winter evenings has by far the greater opportunities.

With regard to the physical advantages of country life modern science has brought statistics to bear. Not a physician can be found who does not preach the value of better air than can be found in cities.

Upon this subject Dr. G. B. Barron, in a paper entitled " Town-Life as a Cause of Degeneracy," read at a recent meeting of the British Association, at Bath, England, said:

" I venture to advance the proposition that the ' vital force ' of the town-dweller is inferior to the ' vital force ' of the countryman. The evidence of this is to be found in a variety of ways. The general unfitness and incapability of the dwellers in our large hives of industry to undergo continued violent exertion, or to sustain long endurance of fatigue, is a fact requiring little evidence to establish ; nor can they tolerate the withdrawal of food under sustained physical effort for any prolonged period as compared with the dwellers in rural districts. It may be affirmed also that, through the various factors at work night and day upon the constitution of the poorer class of town-dwellers, various forms of disease are developed, of which pulmonary consumption is the most familiar. and which is doing its fatal work in a lavish and unerring fashion. Thus it may be conceded as an established fact that the townsman is, on the whole, constitutionally dwarfed in tone, and his life, man for man, shorter, weaker, and more uncertain than the countryman's. I hold the opinion that the deterioration is more in physique, as implied in the loss of physical or muscular power of the body, the attenuation of muscular fibre, the loss of integrity of cell-structure, and consequent liability to the invasion of disease, rather than in actual stature of inch-measurement. The true causes of this deterioration are neither very obscure nor far to seek. They are *bad air* and *bad habits.*

" Taking these causes in the order in which I have placed them, but without reference to their relative intensity, I think *bad air* is a potent factor of enfeeblement. Included in the phrase ' bad air ' are bad sanitation and overcrowding. I have no doubt in my mind that it has a powerful and never-ceasing action, paramount and decisive, on the physical frames

of young and old town-dwellers, producing
deterioration of physique, lowered vitality, and
constitutional decay. For over thirty years I
have been hammering away at this question of
'bad air' and 'bad sanitation' as the prime
causes of impairment of health and race, and
the more I consider it the more I am convinced of the soundness of my conclusions. A
great deal has been said on this subject, and it
is not difficult to adduce conclusive evidence
from a large variety of reliable sources in proof
of the deleterious effects of impure air on the
animal economy. Consumption is the best
type of degenerative action and loss of vital
energy. It stands out in bold relief as the
disease most rife wherever foul air exists. The
significance and value of fresh air were recognized by the old fathers of medicine. Hippo-
crates was accustomed to advise a walk in fresh
air of ten or fifteen miles daily. Aretæus, Cel-
sus, and Pliny speak of the good effect of fresh
air; and our great English physician, Syden-
ham, did the same thing. Dr. Guy found that
of 104 compositors who worked in rooms of
less than 500 cubic feet of air for each person,
12.5 per cent. had had spitting of blood; of
115 in rooms of from 500 to 600 cubic feet,
4.35 per cent. showed signs of consumption;
and in 100 who worked in rooms of more than
600 cubic feet capacity, less than 2 per cent.
had spit blood. Consumption is only one of

the long list of evils to which the town-dweller
is exposed. It may be well to mention that
the Labrador fishermen and the fishermen of
the Hebrides, with plenty of fresh air, are
practically exempt from this disease. The
absence of pure air acts upon the animal economy in much the same way as the withdrawal
of light on plants, the result being pallor and
feebleness of constitutional vigor. This effect
ramifies in every direction; the tissues of
which the human body is composed lose their
tonicity and contractile power, and even mental integrity may be more or less affected. The
pent-up denizens of the courts and alleys of our
large towns, surrounded on every side by im-
perfect light, bad air, and the general aspects
of low life, necessarily degenerate in physical
competency, and their offspring is of a feeble
type.

"The digestive capability of the town-dweller
is of a lower standard and less capable of dealing with the ordinary articles of diet, than the
latter. Consequently town-dwellers live on
such food as they can digest without suffering
—bread, fish, and meat; above all, the last.
The sapid, tasty flesh of animals which sits
lightly upon the stomach, gives an acceptable
feeling of satiety, so pleasant to experience.
Such selection is natural and intelligible, but it
is fraught with danger. I quote from a former
paper: 'The chief diet selected by the town-

dweller begets a condition known to doctors as
the uric-acid diathesis, with its many morbid
consequences.   Pulmonary phthisis and Bright's
disease seem Dame Nature's means of weeding
out degenerating town-dwellers.'   Such are
some of the medical aspects of the case."

Mr. Henry T. Finck, says in his " Roman-
tic Love and Personal Beauty ":

" I am convinced from many experiments that
the value of country air lies partly in its tonic
fragrance, partly in the absence of depressing
foul odors.   Now the tonic value of fragrant
meadow or forest air lies in this—that it causes
us involuntarily to breathe deeply, in order
to drink in as many mouthfuls of this luscious
aërial Tokay as possible ; whereas in the city
the air is,—well, say unfragrant and uninviting,
and the constant fear of gulping down a pint of
deadly sewer-gas discourages deep breathing.
The general pallor and nervousness of New
York people have often been noticed.   The
cause is obvious.   New York has the dirtiest
streets of any city in the world, except Con-
stantinople and Canton ; and, moreover, it is
surrounded by oil-refineries, which sometimes
for days poison the whole city with the stifling
fumes of petroleum, so that one hardly dares to
breathe at all."

THE DANGERS OF CUTTING LOOSE FROM TOWN DRUDGERY.

THE late Matthew Arnold found nothing more characteristic to say about us than that we Americans and our institutions are uninteresting. The length of our railroads, our piles of money, our big buildings, our vast spaces on land and water did not impress him. The human interest was lacking partly because so much of our time or attention and our talk was taken up with these other material matters in themselves not peculiarly interesting. Sir Lepel Griffin, in a harsher review of us and our institutions, says that he would rather live almost anywhere than here, and again he remarks that we are uninteresting. As a nation, we may have attained to a higher level in material matters than the great nations of the Old World; but the work of our public schools in turning out vast armies of pupils, knowing all the same things and viewing every thing from the same

standpoint, necessarily implies monotony. In
our views of what makes a life worth living
there is pretty certain to be a good deal of this
monotony. Ask half a hundred men and
women, taken at random, what makes life
worth living, and certainly the great majority
will say that a life of luxurious idleness offers
the greatest opportunities. At least this is
what they mean, although they will hesitate to
use the word idleness, as contrary to good
morals. Given good health and an ample income, that life is worth living—to the liver at
least—may be considered as sure to follow in
the general estimation of people. Nevertheless
most of us can point out some people who have
health and more money than they know what
to do with, and yet do not live a life which we
consider the best that they could lead.

I will define a life worth living as the one
which offers out-door work and sport, freedom
from anxiety, and plenty of intellectual exercise. I doubt whether a man who passes more
than three fourths of his waking hours in-doors
can remain a healthy animal or get the enjoyment out of life which the mere sense of physical well-being gives. The doctors tell us that

the physical trend of people who live in great
cities is one of steady deterioration; the cities
must be constantly recruited from the country.
To me the persistent city man who never goes
beyond the brick walls and paved streets is entitled to pity very much upon the same ground
as are the animals we see in our menageries.
Centuries of wrong living have evolved a people
who stand confinement and bad air wonderfully
well, but Nature takes her revenge in one way
or another. Nevertheless, we stand our artificial existence so well that most of us forget
that it is an artificial existence. As animals we
ought, by rights, to be in the sunlight from
morning till night. Our ancestors of a few
thousand years ago, who foraged the woods
and waters for birds and fish which they de-
voured raw, slept well in their caves after the
day's chase, and knew nothing of half the ills
we now live in dread of. When Thoreau notes
that the sports of civilized man were the labors
of uncivilized man, does he not indict civilization? Man has given up play as a means of
getting a living. To some extent we go back
to the rational life when we can. The rich
Wall Street gambler, the rich dealer in lard or

leather sometimes goes back to the woods in summer or ploughs the wave in his yacht. But very few of us get rich—perhaps one in a thousand. Is there no way of getting back to a rational life without first winning a fortune, something which comes to so few?

I am aware that here many a reader—provided I am so fortunate as to have many readers —will say : " Oh, we have heard all this before ; it is the old story of moving to the country in order to raise cabbages for a living. It is one more variation upon the ' Ten Acres Enough ' idea." To some extent it is a variation upon that famous book, but with a difference. The hundreds of writers who have taken up the chief idea of " Ten Acres Enough "—the possibility of earning a livelihood by out-door work, gardening, fishing, etc., have, without exception, so far as I know, begun with the assumption that when life becomes impossible in town then the country should be sought. In one case it is the broken-down merchant, tired of meeting notes, tired of the long struggle to ward off bankruptcy, who finally says to himself : " I will sell out my business and with the proceeds buy a strawberry patch, upon which I can raise enough fruit to support my family in comfort." And he does it—in the book. Again, it is the family of the merchant who dies bankrupt who give up their city house in order to find pleasure and profit in keeping cows and selling butter at a dollar a pound—in the book. I have quite a collection of books written by enthusiasts upon country life, and I know some persons who have acted upon the suggestions given, sometimes with very unfortunate results. But invariably this country life is considered as an asylum. So long as a man can live in the city and pay his notes and buy dresses for the family, it is not for him to think of trying the country. The man who falls behind in the race is advised to retreat to the country and take to strawberry raising.

I contend that the strawberry raising or whatever outdoor work is chosen as a means for making a livelihood should be preferred, taken all in all, to the city life even if this city life is fairly successful in a commercial sense, and I hold this for the simple reason that it offers emancipation from some of the worst of city evils, while its drawbacks—and there are drawbacks—are insignificant as compared to

the advantages gained.   Take half a dozen of
the most successful city men you know and
consider (1) How much healthy exercise in the
sunshine they have ; (2) How much of their
life is passed with their children and family ; (3)
How much intellectual exercise do they get out
of life, how many books worth reading do they
open in the course of the year?

In olden times, and in fact in recent times
until the power press and cheap postage appeared, the dweller in the country was largely
cut off from intellectual intercourse.   He had
his few books, as a rule costly and therefore
few, and that was all.   To-day, no matter how
distant the hamlet, the mail reaches it, and for
a trifle the newspapers and magazines bring
him the best thoughts of the world together
with a record of what men who like the fuss
and the noise of towns are doing.   It is no
longer necessary to live with the throng in
order to know what is going on where crowds
meet, and all signs go to show that in the
future it will be still less necessary.   The phonograph, to speak of but one wonder of the near
future, offers extraordinary things to the man
who wants to get away from the crowd.   The

perfected phonograph, and there can be no
reasonable doubt as to its future perfection,
whether this is achieved a year or twenty years
hence, will not only give us books at a cost insignificant as compared to that of ink and
paper, but in a far pleasanter form ; it will be a
pleasant reader always ready to read by the
hour or the day. Not only this, but it will give
us music of any kind—the latest song or the
newest orchestral symphony in a manner to be
enjoyed even by experts. So much has been
accomplished with the phonograph that nothing
seems to be too extraordinary to claim for it.
It is no dream to say that as a means of communicating thoughts and words, the phonograph will do more for the world as an educa-
tor than printing. In the future, authors will
not write their books—they will read them, and
phonographic copies of the result will be so
cheap that our books of to-day will seem ex-
travagantly dear in comparison. With music
it will be the same thing, only that the phonograph will do in this field what it has never
been possible to do before. To provide for the
intellectual food of man was formerly more
difficult than to provide for his physical suste-

nance. To-day it is the other way. In the
future, thanks to electricity, that great power
of coming ages by which the forces of nature
are to be harnessed, food and clothing and
every thing that machinery can make will be
inconceivably cheap. Some thinkers believe
that even by the year 2000 one hour's work a
day will suffice to give a man more comforts
and luxuries than he now earns by eight or ten
hours' work. It will be argued of course, that
what man considers his necessaries will grow
faster than his means for supplying them : in
those favored days to come the day laborer
will deem himself unfortunate if he cannot
dwell in marble halls and eat off gold plate.
Nevertheless there is a point when we can say
that a man is well sheltered from the elements,
well clothed, well fed ; intellectual food in the
shape of books and newspapers will then be so
cheap as to be scarcely worth considering. It
is probable that in those days people will not
herd together at the sacrifice of sunshine and
quiet.

The workman of to-day earns by his day's
labor twice as much food and four times as
much manufactured goods—clothes, tools, fur-

niture—as his father did in the same time.
When we come to books and newspapers the
contrast is more astonishing. The average mechanic can now buy for one day's work more
books than a month's work would have brought
him a century ago, or a year's work would have
brought him in the Middle Ages. More than
that, thanks to cheap postage and circulating
libraries, books are to be had almost for the
asking. One of the things that the Government could do for the intellectual growth of
the country would be to make the postage upon
books almost nominal. This is done in the
case of newspapers, which are sent through the
mails to subscribers for one cent a pound; but
in the case of books, postage is still exorbitant.

That there are certain deprivations in living
in the country, especially in isolation, goes
without saying. First and chief my critics are
pretty certain to note the absence of all society,
certainly a loss if one's position in city life
is such as to give him the society of cultured
people and the time to enjoy such society.
Nor is the raising of cabbages or strawberries
for market by any means a life of luxurious
idleness. Even where, as in my case, the

object is not to earn money, but to save it, there are early hours, soiled hands, and a tired back; some of my friends to whom I have expounded the gospel of idleness, as they call it, although I see nothing of idleness in the raising of cabbages and strawberries, say that just in proportion to my success as a strawberry grower will be my loss in other directions. They say that a day of hard physical labor in the fields will not end with the reading of a good book or magazine article, but in dozing off at eight o'clock. Farmers must keep farmers' hours. I have made some experiments in this field. I have found that whether or not we go to bed at nine o'clock depends wholly upon whether we accustom ourselves to going to bed at that hour. It may require at first some exertion and many yawns to get through a certain book or an article, especially if it is a stupid one, before going to bed. But it will get easier and easier until the day will not seem to be properly wound up without the two hours' reading. The family circle in which reading aloud in not one of the customary evening employments misses one of the great enjoyments of life as well as a potent

means of educating the children. The boy
and girl who learns to know and love the best
books of Thackeray, Scott, and Dickens is pretty sure to have an interest in good reading
through life. But the habit of reading for an
hour every evening and perhaps devoting half
an hour to some standard work not a novel, is
not to be cultivated without some effort, and
some sacrifice in other directions. One of the
most valuable gifts of a liberal education is the
ability to find an interest in books. <u>Unfor-
tunately, but very few people know how to
read.</u> The great number have never learned
when young ; when in middle life their time
has been too much taken up with money-
making ; when the money was made and there
was plenty of time, the faculty of finding
interest in things above every-day detail had
died for want of cultivation.

THE END.

A clever book, right in the main but when
human relationships involving the
social problem are touched upon ex-
ceedingly shallow.

THE
HAND-BOOK DICTIONARY

A Practical and Conversational Dictionary of
the English, French, and German Lan-
guages in Parallel Columns. By GEORGE
F. CHAMBERS, F.R.A. 18mo, roan, pp.
xiii. + 724. $2.00.

"Altogether satisfactory."—*London Times.*

"An excellent hand-book for traveller or student."—
N. Y. Tribune.

"Thoroughly well done. . . . Must prove very
useful."—*Congregationalist.*

"Simple in construction and comprehensive in character."—*Edinburgh Scotsman.*

"It is literally a hand-book."—*N. Y. Critic.*

"To a tourist through France or Germany it is in-
dispensable. It is the best work of the kind that has
come into our hands."—*Indianapolis Journal.*

G. P. PUTNAM'S SONS,

27 and 29 West 23d Street, New York; and
27 King William St., Strand, London.

www.ingramcontent.com/pod-product-compliance
Lightning Source LLC
Chambersburg PA
CBHW020100030726
47498CB00006B/1878